HOLDING OUT FOR LOVE

Windswept Bay, Book Five

DEBRA CLOPTON

Holding Out For Love

Jillian Sinclair needs a man and she needs him now. She dreams of being a mother-but the doctor just gave her the news that if she plans to carry a baby herself then her time is running out. She also wants true love like her sisters but will she have to settle for something less than that in order to get her baby? The last thing she needs is the only man she's loved and lost coming back to town.

Undercover cop, Ryan Locke is back in Windswept Bay but for how long? He broke her heart once when he chose his career over her. Can he be the answer to her prayers or will his dedication to justice take him away from her once more?

CHAPTER ONE

What am I going to do?

Jillian Sinclair blinked away the tears blurring her vision as she knelt in the flowerbed of Windswept Bay Resort, stunned and disbelieving an hour after leaving the doctor's office. Panic clawed at her throat as she rammed a trowel into the dirt, loosening it up just enough for her to plunge her gloved hands into the softened soil. She removed enough soil to make room for one of the many ferns she and her crew were planting as they prepared for the Thanksgiving Day celebration her family always held for the resort visitors and the people of the community.

Thanksgiving…

Jillian squeezed her eyes tight, pausing movement as she struggled to be thankful after learning her hopes and dreams for her future were ticking away by the moment and were very likely already out of her reach.

She struggled to blink away tears that threatened to expose her pain to anyone who might walk up or ask her a question before she got herself composed.

I will not cry. I will not focus on the glass half-empty…

There was so much in her life to be grateful for…she would focus on that.

But the doctor's words throbbed relentlessly, like a migraine in the forefront of her mind… *"Your opportunities for conceiving will diminish substantially in the next couple of years. The endometriosis is too evasive. A total hysterectomy is unavoidable…sooner than later…I'm so sorry, Jillian."*

No more sorry than Jillian. She wanted children. Wanted to conceive them, feel them kick inside her womb, feel the joy of their amazing life growing inside her…wanted to know the love of her baby's daddy, experience that blessed journey with the love of her life.

But there was no love of her life on the horizon.

The only thing on her horizon right now was this bombshell dropped on her this morning.

How could recent, painful female troubles be so devastating so quickly…so unexpectedly? To realize that being able to conceive a child would not be an option for her if she didn't act soon… Her heart squeezed and she felt lightheaded, breathless. *She needed a husband.*

She needed him now, if her dream of carrying a child herself were to come to fruition.

But there are options.

The thought was true. Not her first choice. Her dream was the traditional happily-ever-after choice that her three sisters were living and enjoying right now…she wanted that too.

Sitting back on her heels, she pushed her hair from her face with the back of her gardening glove and let her gaze sweep down the sidewalk to where her crew was getting the soil ready in the larger area of the massive planting. It wasn't just for Thanksgiving but also part of the renovation going on in the rooms on this rear wing of the resort overlooking the beautiful bay. It was a busy time for her as she oversaw the landscaping projects and she loved every aspect of keeping the family resort beautiful for the guests who came here for rest, rejuvenation, and celebrations. Keeping the grounds welcoming and enchanting was a joy to her.

But at the moment, she felt no joy herself.

Planting seedlings and watching them grow and bloom into their full potential was rewarding to Jillian. Watching and helping her children grow into their potential…had been her dream. Motherhood had been her dream. A noise on the second floor drew her attention and she saw Abe, their contractor, help move some plywood into one of the rooms being renovated.

What about Abe?

She and Abe had been out a few times—two times, to be exact. He was a great person. *Could he be her hope?*

She yanked her gloves off and rubbed her temple. He was handsome in a rugged, strong way and a nice guy, but she felt no sparks, no butterflies when she was around him. Jillian *wanted* butterflies.

Her sisters had butterflies in reaction to the loves of their lives. Each had fallen deeply, madly, hopelessly in love in a short period of time. And she was quite certain that butterflies came with the territory. Considering Jillian was the one who had planted hundreds of butterfly bushes in the landscaping that she adored, there was no way on earth that she would settle for anything less than butterflies when it came to falling in love.

Could she settle for less than that for a baby?

In light of the news today, could she hold out for love?

She was happy for her sisters—really, really happy—but her biological clock was ticking just as quickly as Shar, Olivia, and Cali's. *Ha!* Obviously hers was ticking like a time bomb.

"Hey, sis, how's it going?" Shar called, startling Jillian, as she rushed up the sidewalk. Her dark hair and sparkling green eyes were so different from Jillian and Olivia's that it was hard to believe they were triplets. But they were and in every aspect it seemed but reproduction opportunities.

"Great," Jillian lied and plastered a smile on her face, and was relieved that she'd managed to get the tears under control. "What are you up to today?"

Shar beamed. "I'm on a quick mission to see Abe. Gage and I have been working on plans for enlarging the sea turtle hospital with the funds we're donating in his dad's name. I'm here to see when Abe can come over and give us a bid. I'd love to start it before he finishes the resort—if he has time to oversee the two at the same time."

"Oh, that would be good," Jillian said. Shar loved rescuing sea turtles and she'd found a soul mate who shared her passion. She and Gage were perfect together. Made amazingly for each other. Jillian had always called Shar Superwoman because of her dedication and passion for protecting and rescuing sea life and for helping Windswept Bays Sea Turtle Hospital. God had done an amazing job when he created Gage as the perfect partner for her.

Has God created someone for me?

If so, when was he going to show up? Or was she going to have to forget the butterflies and instead, find a good man to father her baby? Abe was a good man.

Shar studied her. "Are you coming to Cali's housewarming?"

Cali's. "Oh," Jillian gasped and sprang from her kneeling position. "I lost track of the time. I need to get home and take a shower and pick up the appetizers I made." She dusted her knees off and was so glad she had prepared the food before she'd lost her mind this morning at the doctor's office.

Shar laughed. "Hey girl, calm down. I'll let them know you're coming. I'll just be here a moment and then I'm heading over. It's all good."

Jillian didn't share Shar's sentiment. All wasn't good at the moment but she was not going to let anyone know she was struggling with bad news. Now wasn't the time. "I'll hurry and see you there."

It was a rushed drive down the beach to her small bungalow on the hillside over one street from the beach, with a glimpse of the ocean from her backyard. Jillian loved the beach but when she went looking for a home, she chose one with room for her flowers and a view rather than direct access to the beach. She threw off her dusty clothes and wound her thick hair into a coil and clipped it up before she jumped into a barely warm shower.

Still breathless an hour later, Jillian parked her car behind a black Dodge in Cali and Grant's drive and breathed a sigh of relief that she wasn't too late. *How could she have forgotten that her sister was holding a special party with her family tonight?* This was a special time for Cali and Grant, her amazing artist husband. They were so very happy and Jillian was happy for them and her other sisters, Shar and Olivia.

Hurrying from the car, and feeling fragmented, she slammed her door and pulled open the hatchback of her small SUV. She pulled out the large, shallow box holding the cake, pie, and appetizers she'd brought. Her four brothers who were here could put away enough food to feed an army, so it took a lot of food—and she did like to bake and cook, so it was nothing for her to go overboard. But several friends were attending the housewarming too, so going a little overboard on preparation was a good thing.

Her hands were full and she had to shift the box to her hip, and held it precariously. Holding her breath and hoping the box held steady, she reached up, grabbed the hatch and pulled downward. The box on her hip shifted.

She gasped and glanced at the Key lime pie and the three-tiered Italian Cream Cake as they slid to one side of the shallow box, shifting the weight. She knew instantly that it was all about to end up on the pavement. She grabbed for it but knew it was too late.

"Oops, I've got it," a man said, diving out of nowhere, his dark head down as both his hands steadied the box on her hip.

Jillian froze as Ryan Locke lifted his gaze to meet her shocked…and horrified…eyes.

Smooth, masculine, and the one man who'd ever caused her heart to ache with young, foolish love. And he was back in town.

The only man ever to rip her heart to shreds and

worse, he didn't even know he'd done it.

Jillian froze as she stared at the man she had never forgotten. She couldn't breathe; she couldn't think as all of her words evaporated. She managed his name. "Ryan."

It took all she had to force his name past frozen lips as memories of the last time she saw him flashed in vivid, mortifying color across her memory.

"It's good to see you, Jillian. It's been a long time."

Nowhere *near* long enough. She wished for the ground to open up and swallow her. She couldn't say anything.

As if not noticing she hadn't said anything, he continued. "I hope you don't mind me dropping in on the party? Jax invited me, and I stopped by and saw Levi at the police department and he invited me, too, so I thought I'd come and say hi to your family."

She cleared the two-ton frog out of her throat. "Oh," she croaked. "Of course I wouldn't mind. Why would I mind?" As soon as the question was out there, she cringed. She knew exactly why he would ask such a question because the last time she'd been in the same room with him, she'd been eighteen and thrown herself at him in the most humiliating way. She felt her cheeks flame and knew she was probably the exact same color as her fuchsia dress.

"Oh, that's great that you and Ryan know each other."

Jillian yanked her eyes off Ryan and felt the flutter of butterflies as she stared in dismay at her friend Blair Baines. Blair was smiling widely at her. She worked for Jillian in the landscape department at the resort. She was also in love with Ryan's cousin Jax, who stood beside her.

As of the last few months, Jax had begun working with Grant, traveling with him sometimes to assist Grant as he painted his world-renowned sea life murals. Jax also owned the Lagoon Adventures in town, a recreation business that did a brisk business in Windswept Bay. They were some of the friends she'd expected to be at this party.

Ryan—she hadn't expected in a million years he would be here.

She thought the world of the younger couple and focused on them as she tried to get a grip on her shock at seeing Ryan for the first time in years. "Yes, we…go way back. Ryan is my brother Levi's best friend." She ventured a glance back at him. He was still as handsome as he'd ever been. His dark-chocolate eyes studied her with butterfly-inducing results. This was not the butterflies she'd just been wishing for earlier. *No, never again where he was concerned.* She yanked her gaze away, disturbed that her pulse careened recklessly and the unwanted butterflies delivered disturbing feelings of that same thrill of attraction that she'd felt as an eighteen-year-old when she looked at the man she'd idolized since childhood.

"Oh, I should have realized that." Blair hugged Jax's arm and beamed up at him. "Jax told me that, duh." She laughed.

Jax grinned. "He's going to run my business while I'm gone to Australia to help Grant with his new mural."

Blair looked sad. "I'm going to miss you the two weeks you'll be gone. But, I'm so glad Ryan could come to help out." She looked back at Jillian. "Jax has been a little stressed lately."

"Hey, I'm fine, Blair." Jax kissed her cheek. "You are the one worrying. This is a great thing for our future."

Jillian felt the love as Jax looked into Blair's eyes. Longing for that kind of love swept over her and she pulled her gaze away and met Ryan's eyes.

Memories hit her like ice water. *Oh and how!* She clutched the box of goodies closer—and decided right then that she might have to hide behind the house and eat every last crumb in hopes to help alleviate her stress.

Blair sighed. "I know, sorry."

The sound of worry in Blair's voice grabbed Jillian's attention. She was one of Jillian's favorite people, and adorably and completely in love with Jax, so what was going on?

"You look great," Ryan said, drawing her attention back to him.

She'd chosen to wear a fuchsia-toned sundress

with silver sandals instead of her jeans and boots hoping the outfit would distract her family from noticing she wasn't feeling up to par. "Thank you," she muttered. "I normally have dirt on my knees and smears across my cheeks."

He smiled, despite her not having meant it to be funny.

"You look awesome, Jillian," Blair said. "That dress looks gorgeous on you."

This was getting awkward.

"You look very nice and do clean up good," Ryan said, a teasing light in his eyes. He'd always loved to tease and she'd lapped up every delightful time he'd focused that teasing on her and not one of her sisters.

"What can I say? I love dirt." The statement didn't come out teasingly as she'd hoped, but sounded nervous—was dirt all she could talk about? How had her day gone from horrible to worse this quickly?

She'd hoped being around her family would be a welcome distraction from her troubles. And now…she wanted to throw the desserts in the vehicle and run away. It was so adolescent that she was embarrassed but even that couldn't change how she felt.

"You always did love to play in the dirt." Ryan joined in again.

He was studying her, smiling…looking as handsome as he always had and holding her secrets behind those nearly charcoal eyes of his.

Her insides trembled. He had witnessed the most humiliating day of her life and then he'd left. Hadn't even said good-bye.

Jillian held his gaze, felt hers harden despite struggling desperately to appear unaffected. She was falling apart and she knew it. "I, I need to get these inside. Bye." She didn't meet anyone's eyes and didn't wait for anyone to say more; no, she just made a beeline for the side entrance of Cali's house.

Somewhere behind her, she heard her brother Jake holler Ryan's name and knew she'd have a little time to compose herself as her brothers cornered him.

He had, after all, been a friend of all of her brothers. He'd been like a sixth son to her parents. And best friends with Levi. And the focus of all of her adolescent admiration.

He was nearly seven years older than her, so much of her life she'd been one of the little sisters. The tagalong. When he'd been a senior in high school, she'd been barely in sixth grade. But just starting to really notice boys and Ryan had gone from being her hero to being her first crush. The problem had been that the crush had never gone away and all through junior high and high school, it had only intensified.

On top of that, Ryan had very nearly begun to ignore her just before when she'd gotten into high school. And then he'd gone off to college and she'd suffered in silence, missing him with all her heart. She hadn't understood why he'd stopped teasing her. She'd told herself it was just because he was older and looking forward to his college life. But when he came home and they ran into each other, he was polite and always seemed ready to get away from her as fast as he could…

Until that night when her prom date had too much

to drink and Ryan had found them, pulled the date off her and then had taken her home. She'd been upset, tipsy, and made the horrible mistake of throwing herself at him. That moment had been the one time in her life she'd regretted to this day.

CHAPTER TWO

His heart raced as Ryan watched Jillian disappear into the house. She hadn't expected to see him. Levi hadn't told her he was in town and it was easy to see she wasn't happy about him being here.

Now wasn't the time to think about the reasons him being back in town would make her cheeks glow nearly purple. Instead, he turned to greet her brother Jake and tried not to think about how beautiful she was. But her sparkling eyes were lodged in his memory and had been ever since that night she'd scared the daylights out of him when she'd thrown her arms around his neck and kissed him as if he'd been her long-lost lover.

He had been her older brother's best friend and she had always been one of his kid sisters…the one who was always peeking around corners at him when she had been a shy fifth and sixth grader and he'd been a junior and then a senior in high school.

She'd been cute and so shy, when her sisters had been outgoing. He'd always had a soft spot for her, wanting to look out for her. Especially considering he didn't get to see his little half-sister, who lived across the state with his mom and her husband. When he'd come home from police academy the week of Jillian's graduation, his whole life had changed. His sister was dead and Jillian had grown up. And that mix of emotions thrown at him from the two events had proved to completely and rigorously change the course of his life.

"It's good to see you, Ryan." Jake grabbed the hand Ryan held out to him and they shook hard while sharing a one-shouldered hug. "Levi said you were coming. We were all glad to know it. It's about time."

All the other Sinclair boys came up behind Jake. All but Cameron, who Levi had said lived on his ranch in Texas and just visited at times.

Trent, Max, and Levi flanked Jake and took turns sharing a handshake and a brotherly hug. Ryan had practically lived with these guys growing up. His own dad had always been working at police headquarters; he had been police chief back then.

They all entered the house, going in through the massive front door. Jax and Blair said they'd catch up with him later and disappeared through the door that led into a large room.

"Levi said you were coming, but we didn't believe him." Max grinned. "We unanimously agreed that until we saw you, we wouldn't believe it."

"It's good to see you, man," Trent said. "And to see you alive. Levi told us your cover was blown."

"And they roughed you up pretty bad," Max added.

Ryan had just recently been able to walk around with just a hint of a limp. His ribs were not completely healed but almost.

"It was not a good experience." He didn't elaborate but he'd almost died. They'd left him for dead and if he hadn't managed to get away while they'd been distracted, they would have finished the job.

Levi crossed his arms and frowned. "They left him for dead."

"But I'm here now. And I'm alive."

"Where were you undercover at?" Max asked, probing.

"Can't say. Just like when you're on a special ops, you can't say."

Max's expression was one of understanding on that. "So your cover was blown—now what?"

That was the question of the decade. "I'm here to relieve Jax at Lagoon Adventures while he goes with Grant to Australia to create the murals he's been commissioned to do and I'll figure it out. I have a desk job waiting for me, if I want it." Which he didn't. He had hopes they'd figure out how to get him back on the front lines in defeating the drug trafficking into the States.

Levi's brow hitched. "You have a job waiting right here, too, anytime you want it, buddy. And it's no desk job."

"Thanks. I'm considering your offer. I really don't know. I don't feel like I've finished what I started and that's my problem right now."

Max was military special ops and he nodded. "I hear you, but all of us here will tell you that you have to look at what you've accomplished because there's always going to be evil to overcome."

"We'll talk," Levi said.

Ryan and Levi had been in the police academy together and had plans to work together. They had chosen the career his dad had, knowing they were never destined to be wealthy. They'd wanted to make a difference but then his little sister had died of an overdose. Ryan's focus had shifted to getting as close to the problem as possible and he had sought to be recruited for undercover. He'd gone deep to avenge his sister's death.

He'd been determined to prevent other kids from dying senselessly because of the lawless actions of drug dealers. He'd committed himself to do what he personally could to fight the war on drugs and that had included going into deep cover.

His thoughts shifted back to Jillian and that night before he'd left to join his team before he'd gone undercover. Before his ideals and the lines of good and evil had blurred…

Before shy, sweet-spirited Jillian had thrown her arms around his neck and kissed him with all her naïve, young heart. And then she'd laid her soul bare by declaring her love for him in a tipsy, alcohol-induced fervor.

Jillian was breathing heavy and probably still red-faced as she rushed into Cali's kitchen. Heat rose up around her face and she felt clammy all over. She was far too young for hot flashes but if this was what they felt like, she didn't want anything to do with them. She set the box of goodies on the beautiful countertop of the large island that separated the kitchen from the large den. The top layer of cake slid to the side but she didn't care.

Cali, Olivia, and Shar stared at her in alarm.

"What?" she asked, trying to figure out how to act normal when Ryan came inside. She had to get a grip.

Shar leaned a hip against the beautiful counter that would make any chef's mouth water. "You're acting weird." *Leave it to Shar to say it like it was.* She leaned forward and stared at her eyes. "And you match your dress."

Jillian gave a nervous laugh.

Cali looked concerned. "You do look a little flushed. Are you feeling okay?"

"Do you have a fever?" Olivia reached out to touch Jillian's forehead.

Jillian pushed her sister's hand away and shot a glance toward the deck, where her mother and her father were watching the sunset. "Don't," she said. "You'll have Mom worried there's something wrong with me."

"Is something wrong with you?" Shar asked.

She could tell them she was coming down with the flu, go home and hole up for a few days. She sure felt as if she were coming down with something. Her upset stomach, her hot cheeks…and the queasiness that came from knowing that Ryan had just entered the other room with her brothers.

He looked so amazing. *That lean jaw and those dark brows over compelling brown eyes.*

Unable to stop herself, she glanced toward the foyer. Her mouth went dry and her hands went damp as a dishrag. And as her brothers and Ryan entered the room, her heart thumped erratically as his eyes met hers.

She spun away and practically dove for the refrigerator. "Is there more food we need to get out?" She yanked open the door and stuck her head in the refrigerator. Heart palpitations had her feeling dizzy as she rammed the gallon of milk with her forehead.

This was ridiculous but she could not help herself. "Do you need pickles?" she called, hoping the cold air would chill her flaming cheeks.

Cali poked her head into the refrigerator, her expression full of alarm. "Seriously, Jillian, what is wrong with you?"

Jillian cringed but remained where she was. "I'm fine."

"Really? Well, Ryan is here and you should go say hi to him. You obviously are tired or something. so you don't need to be helping in the kitchen if cramming your head into the fridge is your version of doing fine."

Jillian refused to give up. She grabbed the jar of pickles. "I want pickles, so others might want them too." Then she marched to the table loaded down with food.

She could feel Cali's eyes follow her. A glance confirmed that all of her sisters were watching her. But it was Olivia whose gaze she caught shifting from her to Ryan. Jillian placed the pickles on the table and then with nothing else to do except run, she turned back to face her sisters. Olivia's brows lifted ever so slightly in question; it was almost like looking into a mirror considering they were identical. There were just some things that sucked when it came to having an identical sister.

She felt as if she'd just eaten bad seafood and then

Shar gasped, having obviously caught Olivia's expression.

Shar grinned. "Good eye, Sherlock," she mumbled for the sisters' ears only. Her eyes were bright with mirth.

Jillian glanced toward Cali as her brows crinkled over her curious eyes. Cali looked around the room toward the brothers, who all stood in front of the fireplace in the large room that overlooked the bay. Grant was being introduced and she saw Levi sharing something funny that made them all laugh as he slapped Ryan on the shoulder. Maybe some old football story or some other mishap they'd all gotten into growing up.

"So that's the way it is," Cali murmured. "And here we've been wondering why you haven't shown more interest in our hunky contractor."

She was talking about Abe. Jillian knew they'd all hoped she would show interest in Abe, and he was hunky, but he didn't make her cheeks blush or her heart race. Not that she was thrilled that Ryan caused that—and more—to create havoc on her emotional and physical well-being.

"Stop, girls. I do not know why all of you keep looking at me and then Ryan. You should probably stop being rude and get over there and say hello to him. I already said my hello before coming inside."

"Cali." Blair led the way from the side hall, with Jax following her. Jillian wanted to hug the girl. "Your home is amazing. Jax showed me around and showed me Grant's studio on the upper floor." The younger woman's peaches-and-cream complexion had a little more color than usual and Jillian suspected a few kisses might have been shared up on that upper floor with its private balcony that overlooked the ocean.

"It's a heck of a studio." Jax grinned as he draped an arm over Blair's shoulders.

"Thank you." Cali, ever the gracious host, focused on her guests. "We put a lot of thought into that space and the light that it would get in the morning, afternoon, and evenings."

As they talked, Jillian relaxed slightly. Until she shot a glance at her other two sisters, who had stepped off to the side and were having a whispering match beside the pantry.

Thank goodness her mom and dad came into the room too.

"Ryan," her mother exclaimed when she saw the man who'd once been in and out of their home like a sixth brother. "Oh my goodness, it's been too long since we've seen you."

Violet Sinclair crossed the room, her face animated and her thick charcoal-gray hair swinging as she hurried Ryan's way and embraced him. Jillian saw the genuine love for Ryan on her mother's face. And on Ryan's too.

And then her sisters went to join the group to welcome Ryan home.

She held back. And then Ryan's gaze met hers over Cali's shoulder as her sister engulfed him in a hug.

Jillian's stomach dropped. *This was going to be so very awkward.*

CHAPTER THREE

Ryan had missed this family. Violet had always welcomed him into her home as if he were one of her own and Sam had been the same way. It had been nice because his dad never remarried after he and Ryan's mother divorced when Ryan was in elementary school. Ryan had seen his mother only a few times a year and so he'd loved spending time at the Sinclair home.

Sam held out a hand and they shook; Sam pulled him into a quick hug. "Been way too long, son."

"Yes, sir. I'm glad to be back home for a while."

"Good." Sam studied him. "I saw your dad the other day. He was heading down to the Keys to fish. Will you be going to join him?"

"I'm not sure, sir. I'm helping Jax out at the moment with the business. I'm going to enjoy my time home. Dad didn't know I was coming and had already booked his season up." His dad had retired and started being a fishing guide at certain times of the year. This was one of those times. Which was fine at the moment because Ryan didn't need him probing for information. Once a cop, always a cop and Alan Locke had not been happy when Ryan had chosen to go undercover. For one, undercover meant he was gone from his family's lives most of the time and he was all the family Alan had. There were fences to mend there and Ryan knew it.

He was glad when Cali came and threw her arms around him in a hug. His gaze locked with Jillian's over Cali's shoulder and he could tell she was still upset and not happy to see him.

Olivia and Shar both got their hugs in and he was quickly brought up to speed on Shar's marriage to

Gage and their work with the sea turtle hospital. And Olivia was soon to be married to BJ, Gage's brother. There was a lot of conversation and when it ebbed, he focused on Grant and Cali and tried not to keep looking at Jillian, who stood on the outer edge of everyone, clearly keeping her distance.

"I want to thank you for taking an interest in Jax. The kid always had talent; he just never knew his potential."

Grant shot Jax a glance. "I'm enjoying helping him develop his talent. I had someone do the same for me back in Texas when I was growing up. It meant the difference in me going into this field and me choosing a different path." He gave Cali a kiss to the temple. "I'm grateful for my art because it brought me to Cali."

"Okay, okay." Jake groaned. "Let's don't get all sappy with the love talk," he teased. "It makes me a little nauseous."

His teasing got him shoves from his brothers and laughter from Jake as his eyes twinkled.

Violet looked at her sons. "You need to take a

lesson from your sisters. None of you boys are getting any younger. I'm just your mother, but I'm thinking it's time for all five"—she shot Ryan a glance—"all *six* of you," she amended her comment, "to start thinking about settling down."

"I think that's a great idea," Shar said above all the other groans of non-agreement and the agreements of her sisters. "Jake, are you seeing that female Coast Guard—"

"Hold off, sis," Jake broke into her comment. "That lasted about five minutes. She was only interested in my body." He chuckled and his mother just shook her head.

Shar groaned. "I don't know whether to believe you or not to believe you."

"Don't believe him," Trent said, sarcastically. "If you saw her, you would know he is not telling the truth. That was one pretty gal. One date with my brother, and she was moving on faster than the helicopter that she flew."

"Hey," Jake snapped. And gave a cocky grin. "I—

"

"It's okay," Shar broke him off. "We don't need to hear the details. We like our happily-ever-after stories more than your snarky remarks." That got chuckles from everybody around her.

Even Jillian laughed.

Shar never had been afraid to speak up. She and Jillian had always been like night and day. He enjoyed the dynamic between the whole family. His family had been disjointed and unconnected in so many ways but the Sinclairs were close. He was closer to Jax than anyone. He felt adrift right now. Distanced in so many ways, he wasn't sure whether he could find his way back. He glanced at Jillian but she'd turned away and was at the food table, cutting slices of pie. Disappointment lodged in his chest. She had no idea that there had been times over the last few years when his thoughts would lock onto her and that last night and her sweet words…and that had been the only thing that had gotten him through the lonely nights and days of pretending to be a part of a drug ring. A pretense that put him on a ledge where lines were gray and sweetness was dead.

Jillian had left the group and started to cut up pies and cakes. But there was only so much to do and finally she had to turn back to the room and join in on the conversations. Thankfully there were so many in the room that avoiding direct conversation with Ryan was easily achievable.

Keeping her eyes off him was not so easy. *Drat her eyes…* That had always been the problem when Ryan had been around: everything else had gone out the window but thoughts of him. *Well, that was not the way it would be now.* She was an adult woman, not a young, infatuated teen.

She scowled and their gazes locked again.

It was time to get some fresh air. She headed toward the patio doors.

"Hey, are you okay?" Olivia asked as she passed her.

"Yes, I'm fine. I just need to make a phone call." She lifted her phone and then headed toward the deck.

Once there, she tried to figure out who she could call because she didn't want to have told Olivia a lie. Plus it was a good excuse to think about something other than Ryan inside the house. Once the sea air surrounded her, she breathed deeply and hoped it would help clear her head. This had to be the worst day of her life.

Okay, where was that positive attitude she'd wanted to focus on? *Gone.*

She moved to the side, out of view of the open windows, and gazed out over the bay. It really was a beautiful place. She was really blessed that she lived here and she never planned to leave. She loved it here. Could forge ahead no matter what…she could. She was strong. She could hold out for love…she could. And she could trust that God had a plan just for her. "Just keep thinking positive," she muttered. "Just keep thinking pos—"

Behind her, the door opened and she stiffened.

"Jillian."

She groaned as Ryan gently said her name. *Think positive.*

She sighed. "Ryan." She tried to keep her voice neutral. Tried to keep the want of acting like a fool out of her voice. "What are you doing?"

"I came to check on you." He nodded his head back toward the house. "You looked upset in there and outside earlier when I showed up. Does my being here bother you? If it's me, I'll go. There's no sense me messing up your evening."

Yes, you bother me in more ways than I'm willing to admit. Please leave.

Jillian fought mixed emotions as his dark eyes held hers. She wanted to run and she wanted to throw herself at him. *Been there, done that, sister—so back off.*

"There is no need for you to leave." The golden rays of the disappearing sun cast a glow over them. Jillian tried not to think of romantic beaches, moonlit walks…but that was hard not to think about with Ryan standing there.

He had witnessed her at her worst and he was probably thinking about that right now as he looked at her.

"Are you upset with me?" His voice was soft, gentle—like a caress.

That angered her. "We know you made it clear the last time we saw each other that you have no use for me." She turned away from him, unable to look him in the eyes.

"You know I didn't mean to hurt you."

His smooth tone rolled over her like silk on warm skin. "You did. Though I'm thankful for it." She squeezed her eyes closed, mortified. "This could really be awkward. I was young and adored you. I humiliated myself by throwing myself at you. I have no one to blame but me. I know that." She'd thrown herself at him, taken him by surprise when she'd kissed him…and then told him she loved him. And he'd treated her like a child.

In reality, she had offered him far more than just her heart: she offered him all of herself. She was eighteen, not as young as she liked to tell herself she was but labeling herself as young helped her feelings anyway.

"You were not yourself," he said.

Heat swamped her again. "I was drunk." That in itself was humiliating. She had never drunk before and hadn't had alcohol since.

"Yes, you were. I'm just glad I was the one you tried those moves on so you didn't make a mistake."

He thought he'd saved her from making a mistake. "Right," she muttered. Anger snapped through her. "You just left." She gripped the railing and fought down emotion that was thick in her voice.

He moved to stand close to her; she fought not to lean back into him. Butterflies lifted in her chest.

"I was doing what was best for you. Everything I did that night was for your own good. I didn't even think you would remember what you did."

Oh, she remembered. "I was eighteen. I was not a child. I was old enough to know what was good for me and what was not good for me." *What was she saying?* "And besides that, you left the next day and never even said good-bye. I had bared my soul to you and you didn't even tell me good-bye."

His brows dipped and his dark eyes dug into her.

"Jillian, I lost my sister a month before that night. She was your age. When I looked at you and your sisters, I saw Jen. I needed to find a way to try to stop other kids and young people from dying from the drugs that scum were bringing into this country. I was humbled by what you were offering me but I could only think about stopping more pain and anguish happening for families. I'm sorry you were hurt."

Jillian told herself to stay angry. She told herself to let it all go. Obviously he'd only ever thought of her as a little tagalong sister of his best friend. To him, she had just been a drunk kid.

Suddenly, Ryan leaned in and kissed her cheek and then before she could blink, he stepped back and stared at her with eyes that bore through her and shook her to her very core.

"I'll see you later, Jillian. I wish only the best for you. If anyone asks, tell them I had to leave early." And then he walked off the deck and disappeared into the very dusky evening along the path that led around to the front of the house. Jillian just stood there as her heart raced and her pulse pounded.

And those unwanted butterflies caused havoc inside her.

Her life was in enough turmoil right now. Ryan coming back to town and reminding her of the most humiliating night of her life was not what she needed. Knowing that he'd believed she was too young and drunk to know what she'd been doing that night gave her some relief from her humiliation. But that was also the problem: she hadn't been too young. And she hadn't been as drunk as he believed she'd been…

Ryan couldn't get away from Jillian fast enough. As he strode through the beautiful landscaping of her sister's home, that he assumed Jillian had had her talented hands involved in, he tried to focus. Not on how beautiful and lovely she was but on his career. He was going back undercover if they'd let him. He was simply here to take the mandatory time off before he was evaluated again.

Jillian represented everything clean and wholesome that he was striving to preserve. Every lead he'd been able to give his narcotics team, every life they'd been able to save by taking drug deliveries off the streets had been worth the life he'd chosen. Jillian represented the untouched kids he'd been striving to save. His sister had represented those lost. *And Marla*... His heart hardened as he thought of Marla. She represented what no one caring enough to step in could result in.

Marla had blurred the lines for him. His heart ached for her even while he felt betrayed. *What had he expected?*

He reached his truck and climbed inside. He gripped the steering wheel. He needed to get away from Jillian, and he needed to stay away from her. She was too good for the man he'd become.

Shame and filth clung to him from his undercover work. He'd come home in hopes of getting his head screwed back on straight so they'd release him to work again. He didn't want to be sitting behind a desk. He wanted to be in the middle of things.

But as he sat there struggling with the load on his shoulders, he wondered why Jillian was not married. *Why didn't she have an adoring husband and a couple of sweet kids like her running around?*

CHAPTER FOUR

His first morning helping Jax out at Lagoon Adventures went by fast. Ryan had helped one person after another rent a kayak and start on their adventure down the lagoon. By lunchtime, he'd hardly stopped. There was a lull in the arrivals as people either took lunches with them and stopped somewhere along the lagoon to eat or they had lunch first and then came for an afternoon excursion. He was filing release forms when Levi looked around the corner.

"Hey, got time for lunch?" He held up a bag that had Ryan's stomach growling immediately.

"Is that what I think it is?"

"Oh, yeah. I figured if you could eat, we'd have some of Juan's tacos."

"I'm all in." Ryan grinned and marched straight to the picnic table that sat on the edge of the deck that overlooked the lagoon. Juan's roadside taco stand had been in Windswept Bay for as long as Ryan could remember. It had been a favorite of the guys all through school. "Glad you got to show up. More so now that you've brought Juan's."

He and Levi had set up a tentative lunch date today but with Levi being the chief of police, there was never a guarantee that he could show up at a certain time.

"It's pretty dead today, so it all worked out."

"It hasn't been dead here, that's for certain. I'm starving and had decided food was out of my reach if you didn't show up because I can't leave right now. I forgot how busy this place is."

"Yeah, that's how Jax stays so in shape." Levi patted his stomach and sat down across the table from Ryan. "I have to hit the gym to keep in shape but the kid gets a workout working here."

"Yeah, tell me about it. I'll probably have tight hamstrings in the morning. I've been up and down so much today. On the other hand, my ribs aren't complaining so that means they're healed up as far as I'm concerned."

"Good. Then you can compete in the Thanksgiving Day obstacle course challenge with me."

He laughed. "Your family still holds that?"

"We sure do. We feed anyone who wants to come out that day and then we let the kids play and we compete."

"I'm in then. But I can't guarantee how I'll do."

"It'll be good for you. Your cousin is a good guy."

"I think so. It seems like he's got a good gal too. Blair seems really sweet."

"According to Jillian, she's great. She's been working with Jillian in the landscaping part of the resort for the last year and she loves her to death."

Ryan shot Levi a rueful eye. "Jillian likes everyone." *Almost*—she wasn't liking him too much anymore.

Levi chuckled. "True. It takes a lot to get on her bad side."

Ryan took a bite of taco. "Yeah," he grunted. "That's very true. Why are you still single?" he asked, trying to change the subject. He'd rather ask why Jillian was still single but bit back the need and asked about Levi instead.

Levi hitched a brow. "I could ask you the same thing, but I think I know. Your life makes you leery of relationships. Undercover work is rough on a family man."

"Bingo." Ryan hid his emotions behind a poker face. He was a master of hiding what he was thinking. He'd had to be; his life had depended on it.

"I know you went undercover because you needed to feel like you were doing something more to stop the drugs that killed your sister. I get that. But don't you think you've been under long enough? Four years of basically living your life as someone you're not is highly irregular. How did your cover not get blown before now? My gut tells me you've been involved in some significant takedowns over the last four years."

True. Thugs he'd had to pretend were his friends. Scams he'd ratted out and stayed out of during the takedowns so his cover would stay hidden. He thought of Marla and rubbed his temple. He'd tried to help her…tried to save her…and in the end she'd lost her life too.

"You look bad," Levi said. "You look beyond your years. Don't you think it's time to get your own life? Or is that why you're on leave?"

Ryan wadded up the empty wrappings of the tacos that he'd devoured and stuffed them into the empty paper bag. "They don't want to send me back in. I'm not sure what I want." Ryan gave him a skeptical look. "You never answered my question. Why aren't you married? You live in paradise—you're surrounded by women. And you're the police chief, for Pete's sake. You can't tell me you're not in high demand."

"Hey, this job might not be undercover, but it's demanding. No time for building a lasting relationship."

"You have deputies, don't you?"

Levi looked serious. "I do. But the truth is we're

out here on the edge of boring to most officers. We're not exactly a metropolis. New recruits are usually looking for more action than a laid-back resort town dealing with tourists. It's not really the place to move you up in outside opportunities. So I have a few really talented officers and I have an abundance of officers just waiting out retirement, so that keeps me busy. If I do get star talent, they're just waiting for something better to come along."

"And leave you stranded."

"Right. They want something exciting. The most exciting things we've had in the last few months is the paparazzi came to town twice. Once because of Grant and last month because of Olivia. I am not a fan of that nonsense. But the truth is, no town is without problems and it takes diligence to keep it down. You'd be valued here. I'm just putting that out to you."

Ryan didn't like thinking about this beautiful place having problems. "So you don't see a lot of drugs coming through the coast?"

"We've been lucky not to have what everyone else has."

"You and I both know that's due in part to you."

"You and I both know I need help. Good help. Someone who is smart enough to stay ahead of the situation before it happens. You have a job waiting if you want it. I'm actively recruiting you as of now."

Ryan studied the lagoon, mulling over his options. His entire life felt up in the air. "I'll keep that in mind. Thanks for the offer."

"I think it would be a win for all of us. You and the people of Windswept Bay."

A couple came around the corner.

"Can we get a kayak?" The older man tugged at the woman's hand.

"Is it safe?" she asked.

"Yes sir, you can get a double or two singles. And it's safe. You'll have on a life vest too." Ryan stood. "Looks like my break is over and back to work for me."

Levi grinned. "I guess I'd better do some work too. We'll be talking."

Ryan gave him a thumbs-up and watched his friend leave before he turned to the couple. The woman in her sixties needed reassurance. He smiled and went to help her.

But his thoughts went to Jillian. *Would she thaw toward him if he stayed?* He told himself he needed to put her out of his thoughts. That it was best that she be mad at him and that she keep her distance. She'd said he hurt her…and that hurt him to know but he'd done what he needed to do.

Should he keep his distance? Could he keep his distance?

He was finding it hard to get her off his mind and he wasn't certain what he was going to do about that.

Four days after learning her dreams of a baby were in jeopardy—and of seeing Ryan for the first time since she was eighteen—Jillian was busy at work. Work was her saving grace.

She'd been working in the flowerbed when Abe had asked her to come take a look at the remodel. Now she stood beside Abe as they surveyed the new bathroom remodel. All the rooms would have them.

And Abe's crews were working hard on downsizing the bedrooms and enlarging and luxuriating the bathrooms. Thankfully, when the rooms had first been built, they'd been larger than the average hotel room, thus they could handle the lost square footage. And the modernized bathrooms would be loved by the customers.

"You're doing a great job, Abe. It's everything we've been hoping for and more."

"I'm glad you think so. The crew has done a really good job."

It wasn't lost on Jillian that Abe was not only handsome and nice, but he was also modest. He always gave his crew the credit they deserved. She liked that. She met his gaze. *Please let me feel something. Just a few butterflies.* But no, there was nothing more than the knowledge that he was a nice man she liked and respected.

No butterflies, no quickening pulse, no weak knees: nothing. It was enough to make her go buy a gallon of her favorite pralines-and-cream ice cream and eat the entire bucket in one sitting. And sadly, the grocery store was between here and her home. It was going to be hard to pass up.

She lifted her gaze to Abe's lips and imagined kissing him…no, no tingles. *Nothing like what happened the instant Ryan came near—*

Abe cleared his throat. "Jillian, are you okay?"

Her gaze shot to his; he hitched a brow.

"What?" She gasped and cringed inside, knowing he'd caught her ogling his lips.

"Do I have something on my mouth?"

"No, I mean— Sorry, I, I was lost in thought. Didn't realize I was staring. So..." She cleared her throat. "What did you want to show me?"

He didn't look as if he completely believed her, but he moved to a wall. "If you and your sisters want it, I can put a small bookshelf here in this wasted space left by making the coffee bar around the corner. It would add a little more adventure to the room. Or we can wall it up. I just wanted to float the idea to you."

"Great idea." *She needed to get out of there.*

He crossed his arms. "Okay, if you think the three of you would like to see this, I'll work up an estimate.

It won't be much."

"I think they'll love it." She edged toward the door.

"Fine. I'll work up a firm cost sheet tonight. Are you sure you're okay?"

"Good. Perfect. I mean, I'm fine." *He* was perfect. If he was attracted to her, she could settle for a perfect man like him…right? If it meant making her dreams of babies come true—*couldn't she?* Ryan filled her thoughts like an unwanted mealybug in her flowerbeds. "Thanks. I've got to go." She waved, spun, and fled.

An hour later, she wheeled her car into the grocery store parking lot and screeched to a halt. She hurried inside and practically ran to the ice cream aisle. She'd buy not just one but three gallons of the frozen dessert she was so utterly stressed out.

Abe was the perfect man and she should be doing everything in her power to turn his head and get his attention so she'd have a shot at a baby. But no, her thoughts kept going to Ryan. It had taken her months to get over not only humiliating herself that night by declaring her love for him but also to assure herself that she'd really not loved him. Not really.

But despite convincing herself of that, no other man had ever measured up to the pedestal that she'd placed him on. And now, he was back.

"Pralines-and-cream, here I come," she muttered, as she wheeled her cart down the center of the freezer cases. When she got there, she yanked open the glass door and grabbed the first gallon and placed it in the buggy. She was reaching for the second gallon when, of all people, Ryan walked up. *Could this day get any worse?*

He leaned against the glass case, crossed his arms over his broad T-shirt-clad chest and grinned. "So pralines-and-cream is still your weakness." His eyes crinkled at the edges.

"I'm just buying some ice cream. Do you have a problem with that?" She glared at him, feeling every bit the shrew.

He held his hands up and frowned. "Nope. I was just teasing. But I see my mistake." He reached for a gallon of pralines-and-cream and let the door close as he placed it in his buggy; then he walked away.

Jillian stood there, feeling horrible, and watched him casually push his cart toward the end of the row. This was not her—this mean, grumpy person. He had apologized for hurting her the other night. Not that that could erase all the hurt she felt but it wasn't his fault she'd gotten a crush on him and then thrown herself at him.

She moved forward, pushing her buggy as quick as she could. "Ryan," she called.

He stopped and pivoted toward her. "What, Jillian?" he asked, sounding frustrated himself.

What had she planned to say? He cocked his head slightly when she didn't say anything at first but he kept quiet. Clearly, the ball was in her court. "I don't normally act like this."

"I know you didn't used to act this way. I'm sorry if I had a part in changing you."

She sighed and all the pent-up anger and hurt going on inside her crashed at her feet. "It's not you. Not really. I have a lot going on—"

"Look." He reached to the small rack at the end of

the row and picked up a bag of plastic spoons. "I just happen to have a carton of ice cream and an entire bag of plastic spoons. Would you go with me somewhere and share it with me and maybe we could talk? Maybe we could start over?" He waved the spoons like an olive branch, a peace offering. A way to move past the anger.

Jillian's insides trembled. "Yes. I'd like that."

He smiled and her day seemed a little brighter. "That's the best thing I've heard since I arrived back in town." He looked at her cart. "Do you think we need your two gallons and my single?"

She smiled. "Maybe I'll put mine back."

"Sounds like a plan. I'll wait right here."

All the way down the row, she felt him watching her and she felt the hum of anticipation singing through her as the voice inside her head started to chant, "Keep calm and proceed with caution."

A few minutes after running into Jillian buying ice cream, Ryan led the way to a picnic table at a small park that overlooked the sparkling bay. The park was a popular place but he found a table off to the side and set the carton of ice cream on the table. Families played on the beach but the wide span of sand kept them out of the hub of everything, giving them a semblance of privacy. He was happy at the unexpected turn of events. Having been feeling down as he'd gone to the store to buy something to help ease his worry, he'd never expected to find Jillian there.

The sun-bronzed late afternoon sky sent golden rays reflecting off the blue waters, making it a stunning day. But nothing was more stunning to him than Jillian.

They sat on the same side of the picnic table so they could face the water, though she left ample room between them. He was just glad she was here.

"I'm thinking this is going to be amazing." He took the lid off the ice cream and then reached in the bag and pulled out a spoon and offered one to her.

"Thank you." She looked out at the water. "It's beautiful here." She smiled at him and nearly took his breath away.

Jillian had grown into a beautiful woman, with her soft honey-blonde hair and delicate features. But she'd always been a pretty girl with a gracious and sweet spirit about her. "I think so too." He couldn't help staring at her. "I still remember the first time that we discovered that we both loved the same ice cream. It was the summer before your senior year in high school and we were all at a Fourth of July celebration your parents were throwing. They were teasing you for not being a 'normal' girl in love with chocolate."

"I remember that. And you said it was your favorite too." Jillian smiled again. "I remember being surprised that a guy liked ice cream with candied pecans and caramel."

He laughed. "I guess it's not the most masculine-sounding ice cream."

"Maybe not but it's the best."

He dipped his spoon into one side of the softened dessert and took a bite. Jillian did the same on the other side of the carton. The flavors of vanilla, caramel, and brown sugar-coated pecans filled his mouth. "Yup, it is still the best."

"It is. And when it's soft and creamy, it's unbeatable." She took another spoonful and smiled as she took the bite.

They ate in companionable silence for the next few moments. Finally, he paused. "Jillian, I owe you an explanation."

"Not really. I mean, you had no idea your best friend's kid sister thought she was in love with you. You hadn't done anything to bring that on. You were always just you, a really nice guy. That night was just a real mess." She dipped the spoon into the ice cream and stirred the quickly melting treat. "I was young and naïve. I'm ever grateful that you turned down my…offer. I'm mortified that I made such an advance at you. You were so stunned when I practically attacked you."

Her cheeks were pink now as she spoke and he could only imagine how embarrassed she must feel remembering that moment when she not only smothered him in kisses, but told him she loved him and offered to sleep with him. It had scared the daylights out of him.

This was Jillian, after all.

Nice, shy Jillian. And she'd been out of control.

The one person he'd never expected to make him a proposition and she'd done it.

"You were not you that night. We both know that."

She nodded and took a quick bite of ice cream.

"I cared for you, Jillian."

She set the spoon down and stiffened. "I'm sure you did. I was the kid sister. One of four. And your reaction was exactly as it should have been—"

He placed a hand on her arm. His pulse kicked in at touching her. "I *cared,* Jillian."

"Yes, I know. But I shouldn't have expected you to feel more. What did I know? I was too young anyway."

"Jillian, I cared about you," he said firmly, trying to get through to her. "I just had so much that had happened. I was leaving. I was going…undercover. I had nothing to offer you and you deserved so much more."

She stared at him, her eyes muted with confusion.

Or disbelief.

"I needed you to know I cared. You are a very special woman. I've always thought so. I had too much going on in my life back then and you were young. I had set in motion the destination of my life and for me to tell you I cared would have been unfair to you."

She looked stunned. "You cared?" she repeated cautiously. "As in, cared in a romantic way? Not in a 'you're my best friend's tagalong little sister' cared?"

He smiled, not at all sure where this conversation was going or what she was thinking. "I did. But nothing would have been gained by me telling you that. My hope was that you moved on, found love and have had a wonderful life."

Jillian's brows crinkled over puzzled eyes. "I have moved on. That was a long time ago."

"Then why have you been so angry with me?" *Why was he pushing? He should let it go.*

"Because I was embarrassed you didn't tell me you were leaving. You just left. Levi told us later that you'd gone deep undercover. We knew it had to do with your sister's overdose. But I guess I thought you could have told me that night you were leaving."

His heart thumped hard and heavy in his chest. "You were worried about me?" He'd told himself she simply had a schoolgirl's crush on him back then.

"You were practically part of our family. Of course we were worried about you. And then I was angry at myself and embarrassed and mortified. But, then you never came back."

She studied him and unease filtered through him. Jillian didn't need to be exposed to the world that he had been involved in for the last few years. "There was no need to worry about me. I was doing what I needed to do and it was…not a life I could share. Or would want to get anyone involved in." He paused, wanting so much to tell her that he cared. Until now, he hadn't understood completely how much he cared. "You didn't need to be involved with someone like me. I thought you'd wake up and realize you'd had a bad night and move on. I am really surprised you haven't married and had kids."

She blinked and her beautiful eyes dimmed. "No, not so far." She blinked again as she looked out toward the kids romping on the sand.

"I can't believe that. Are the men here crazy?" Something didn't feel right. *Was that tears she kept blinking away?*

"I date." She stood. "I guess we better throw this away before it makes a huge mess." She reached for the melted ice cream in the carton and he did the same. Their hands collided, knocking it to the ground.

"Sorry," he said, stooping quickly; she did the same and they bumped heads. "Now I'm really sorry."

"It's okay. We're both hardheaded." She laughed and rubbed her forehead as he scooped the carton up before its contents completely poured out onto the sand.

Their eyes met and he wanted so much to kiss her in that moment. Instead, he stood and moved to the garbage can and turned his back as he stuffed the carton into the can.

"Did you find someone while you're gone?"

Her question took him by surprise. He stiffened and thought of Marla. "No," he said. "My work wasn't conducive to relationships." He turned to face her.

She nodded and the air seemed charged with electricity as they studied each other. *He wanted…* He shook himself and shut down that thought. "I just wanted to get things right between us. To make sure you knew you had nothing to be embarrassed about. I don't like knowing you're angry with me."

"We're good. Pralines-and-cream heals all wounds." She laughed softly and it dug deep into the dark corners of his heart. "Are you going back? I mean, after Jax gets back?"

"I don't know. To be honest, my cover was blown. I don't know where I'm going next or what I'm going to do. So, you're dating someone now?"

"I'm…yes," she said, after hesitating. "Abe, the contractor at the resort. We've been out a few times."

His mood dimmed. "Then, that's good."

"Yes. Good."

They walked out toward the parking lot in silence. When they reached her car, he opened the door for her and she turned toward him. They were close; their gazes locked. He couldn't help himself. He bent and kissed her cheek and then stepped back. "You take care of yourself, Jillian. I'll see you around."

She nodded. "I'll be here." She got into her car and pulled the door closed. She met his gaze through the window and then she drove away.

He swallowed the lump in his throat as he watched her disappear down the street.

She deserved more, better than the man he had become and he knew it. But it took everything he had in him not to go after her.

CHAPTER FIVE

S he hadn't slept.

Not one little wink…and Jillian was feeling it as she entered the office the next morning. Cali, Olivia, and Shar were huddled in deep conversation around the coffee machine and instantly looked guilty when they saw her. They were all supposed to be meeting to discuss the upcoming Thanksgiving Day celebration but in all honesty her heart couldn't celebrate, no matter how hard she tried.

Jillian strode into the mix, grabbed a mug and filled it with coffee…her fourth of the morning. Yes, she'd already had three cups at her house after tossing and turning, her mind warring over what to do with her life. Giving up, she'd crawled out of bed and brewed a pot of coffee and headed to the back deck. And there she'd sat, *alone,* drinking cup after cup of coffee in her charming garden beneath a romantic starlit sky, watching moonlight dance over the shimmering water.

"We're glad you're here." Cali sounded nervous. "We wanted to talk to you."

Jillian sank into her desk chair and took a cautious sip before she looked up to connect with her sisters' varying looks of dismay and worry.

"Something is wrong," Olivia said. "We're worried about you."

"I'm fine." But Jillian knew she wasn't. She should have been adjusting to the news from the doctor but she wasn't. A heaviness hung over her that felt like quicksand pulling at her.

"No, you're not." Shar's eyes flashed. "You look ragged and you have your shirt on inside out. That is not fine."

Jillian glanced at her T-shirt. "Well, that's a

bummer."

"Okay." Olivia came over; her sisters trailed behind. "That does it. What is going on?"

"Yes, honey," Cali said, concern etched across her delicate features. "You've been acting unlike yourself for days. Ever since my party. I know we've been busy and you've been out there working on the landscape, but we've been watching. And I haven't forgotten that you were redder than your favorite rose that night at the party. And you practically climbed into my refrigerator. That isn't the calm, cool, and collected Jillian we all know."

"*And*," Shar jumped in. "We saw you on the porch with Ryan. Then he left early. And you did too. Is there something going on between you two and you are afraid to tell us?"

That startled her.

Shar gasped. "There is! I knew it."

"No, there isn't," Jillian denied. But she knew it was no use. She'd felt weird, disconnected ever since talking to the doctor and now Ryan was constantly on her mind. She had a great fear that she was about to do something totally and completely off the wall if she didn't talk to someone. If she didn't let someone talk her off the ledge.

"Now why do I not believe you?" Cali asked. "Ryan is a great guy. You used to idolize him growing up."

"You did," Olivia agreed. "You never said so but we all knew it was true. You never took your eyes off him when he was around."

So much for keeping secrets from her sisters.

Shar smiled. "I think we all probably had a crush on him at some point. Only you still have one, don't you?"

"Okay, yes. I used to have a crush on him. But seven years is a lot of age difference."

"In school," Shar retorted. "Not in the adult world. It's a perfect age difference."

"It is. And if you still like him, you and Abe have just gone out a few times. Is that worrying you?"

Jillian set her coffee down. "No. That's not it." She rubbed her temple, where her head had started to throb. She hadn't said the words out loud yet. Only the doctor had said the words out loud. *What—did she think if she kept them inside and hidden that they wouldn't be true?*

She looked at Cali. "I just found out, the day of your party, that I may not be able to have children." Her sisters gasped as she continued, "*And,* if I am able to have children, I need to have them sooner, not later. Like now."

The room went silent as her sweet sisters paled. They knew how much she wanted kids.

Cali's eyes welled with tears. "Why didn't you tell us? You've known this all week?" She wrapped her arms around Jillian. "I'm so sorry."

Jillian's heart squeezed tight and she fought down the emotion knotted in a tight fist inside her. A tear slipped out of her eye and rolled on her cheek anyway.

"Why?" Olivia asked. "I'm so sorry, but why is the doctor saying this?"

"There was a long list of reasons, as it turns out. But, it boils down to the fact that my endometriosis is strangling the life out of my ovaries and just being a bully. And there are some other problems that are only going to get worse. And quickly. It's just not good."

There, she'd said it.

Shar hadn't said anything and Jillian glanced at her usually blunt sister, who was unusually silent.

Jillian swiped a tear away with her fingertips. "I keep trying to focus on all the blessings that I have and that there still is a chance. And that I can adopt. But, I wake up every morning and can barely make myself get out of bed. Every moment that I'm not trying to have a baby is lost time."

"You need a man." Shar finally spoke. "And you need him yesterday."

Jillian stared at Shar, startled that she was saying the exact words that Jillian's heart kept telling her.

Cali shot Shar a frown. "Don't tease her at a moment like this."

Shar looked unaffected. "I'm not teasing. I'm stating a fact."

"Well," Olivia said, cautiously. "You do have a point. But, really Shar, now is not the time—"

"Now is exactly the time," Shar disagreed. "She is running out of time. Didn't you hear her?"

Jillian watched her sisters having the battle that had been warring inside her head for a week.

Sympathy filled Cali's eyes. "Jillian, you don't need to be desperate. I mean, you're gorgeous; you're a sweet and amazing person—which is the most important thing. A man will come along and be so blessed to have you for a wife and mother of his children. God's got this."

"Right," Olivia said. "There is someone special out there for you. Ryan is back in town."

"He's an undercover agent," Jillian finally managed to say.

Olivia frowned. "Right. But he might not go back. And Abe!" she exclaimed. "He's still in the picture and amazing."

"He is a great guy. He's perfect but I don't…feel anything special when I'm with him."

Her sisters stared at her.

"That would be a problem," Shar said. "You have got to feel sparks and butterflies and goose bumps."

"Love. She's got to feel love," Cali admonished Shar.

"Hey, back off, big sis. I totally believe love is number one. But all that other comes into play too."

Jillian took a deep breath.

"Maybe if you spend more time with Abe?" Olivia continued, looking hopeful.

"What do you feel when you're around Ryan?" Cali asked, a glint in her green eyes.

Jillian felt her cheeks burn. She stood up at the thought of Ryan that first evening when he showed up at Cali's house and then again sitting at the picnic table eating ice cream. She had felt undeniable chemistry with Ryan. She tried not to think about her humiliating display of desperation the night of her prom.

Shar laughed. "If her flaming cheeks are a sign, then there are definitely fireworks. That explains why you nearly crawled into the refrigerator at Cali's."

"It's true." Jillian cringed. "So true and I just don't know what to do."

"You spend time with him," Olivia said.

"Right." Cali placed her hands on her hips. "Girl, you come out of your shell. He kept his eyes on you, too, so don't think this is one-sided. I saw the way he kept looking at you."

Butterflies fluttered just thinking about that. "But it's just not that easy. I can't in all good conscience not tell someone I date that I may not be able to have a baby. And isn't that the perfect thing to say on a first date?"

Shar cringed. "Oh, that is a problem."

"Not with Ryan," Cali defended. "He's practically part of the family."

"I can't do it." Jillian glared at her sisters. "Don't think I haven't been thinking about this. It's driving me crazy. I'm desperate but…I don't think I can tell a man up front how desperate I am. And I can't not tell someone for fear he will fall for me and then learn I can't give him a baby. It's horrible."

Finally, all three of her sisters were speechless.

She had thought of all of this. And somewhere under that romantic moon last night, she'd known what her only option was. "So…I'm going to start looking into a donor bank. I think that's the best thing."

"No," her sisters yelped in unison.

Cali crossed to her and cupped her face. "You

need to take a deep breath and just pray about this. You, my sweet sister, need to find peace. And then see what happens. Just be you for now."

Olivia came and put an arm around her waist. "It's going to be okay. Cali is right."

"Group hug." Shar flung her arms around them all. "One for all, and all for one. We are with you, sister. And no matter if you can or if you can't have babies, any man who is blessed to get you for a wife is the luckiest man alive. And don't you forget it."

Jillian cried then. "I love you three. You're the best sisters ever." And it was true. Somehow she'd forgotten that she wasn't traveling this road alone.

"Yes, I'll be ready. It sounds fun." Ryan held the phone between his shoulder and chin as he lifted a kayak onto a multi-tiered rack. It was closing time and he was ready for a jog. More than ready.

Levi chuckled on the other end of the line. "You may not think fun when we're done. Are you sure you're healed up enough for the challenge?"

"Once again—I said I was in for the Thanksgiving Day Obstacle Course. Are you trying to talk me out of it? Starting to think we'll lose?" He hoped not because Ryan was looking forward to competing.

"Of course I haven't. I'm just making sure you're up to it. This will be like old times," Levi said. "Talk to you later."

Ryan hit End on his phone and then finished closing up and headed home to his dad's place to change before taking a jog. His hip was better but he needed to keep it limbered up. He was lucky the bullet hadn't shattered his hip or hit a major artery when his cover had been blown.

He was ready to get off. Needed to get off. Everyone who'd come in today had been couples who had the look of love all over them. They'd not seemed capable of keeping their lips apart and letting their love shine—and he'd been front and center watching, with Jillian on his mind.

He needed a run. He needed to work off some steam.

What he wanted was to see Jillian. But that was a

bad idea, so a nice, long jog on the beach was what he needed.

Since watching her drive away from him after they shared ice cream, he had been this way and it was just getting worse.

Thirty minutes later, he was jogging down the beach when he noticed a huge crowd gathered. Curious, he headed that direction. When he reached the edge of the crowd, he spotted the sea turtle hospital ambulance and Shar's familiar dark head at the center, near the water's edge. Gage was there, too, along with several people wearing shirts with the turtle hospital's logo. He moved to get closer when he noticed Jillian. His pulse kicked up several notches and the day suddenly seemed brighter just looking at her. She was like a ray of sunlight…and he couldn't help being drawn to her.

He made his way through the crowd until he stood beside her. "What's going on?"

"Ryan," she said, clearly startled to find him there. Her big green eyes were wide with excitement. "It's release day. The sea turtle they rescued here several months ago is being released back into the ocean. It was in bad shape when they rescued him and they really never expected to be able to set him free again. But he's doing fantastic and gets to go back to his home. Do you want to help? I'm supposed to be up there."

"Sure," he agreed, realizing she could have asked him whether he wanted to walk on hot coals and he'd have agreed.

"He was rescued here in the bay, near the resort." She led the way through the crowd. "And they always try to release them near where they were found. It's so wonderful when they get to go home, back into the ocean they love."

"It's been a long time since I've participated in one of these." He smiled, liking the work that the hospital did for the sea turtle life in this area. "I remember Shar was crazy about helping out the sea turtle hospital all those years ago, so it looks like she's continued her work."

"Oh yes, she's driven by purpose." Jillian smiled. "Hey, Superwoman," she called, waving to Shar.

"Hey, come on and help us." Shar waved from where she, Gage, and two other men held the edges of a large container that a good-sized sea turtle sat in.

He followed Jillian. She greeted everyone and grabbed the edge of the container. "John, Alex—this is Ryan," she said in quick introduction to the two men he didn't know.

They exchanged quick greetings. Gage smiled. "Hey, good to see you. This is dangerous. You might get hooked like I did."

"Maybe so," he said.

"Let's do this," Shar instructed and then they were walking.

They all carried the open-ended tub to the water and walked into the chest-high surf. It was heavy and the turtle wasn't the biggest he'd ever seen but it wasn't a lightweight either. Jillian's grip slipped when she stumbled in the surf. He held tight to the tub with one hand to take her slack and reached out to steady her. "You okay?"

Water splashed over them all and she laughed as she grabbed the tub again. "Yes, fine. Thanks for the save. I almost took a swim with the turtle."

"Anytime." He grinned at her, loving the joy that sparked in her eyes. He realized some of that had been missing when they spoke and he wondered whether he was the cause of it.

"Okay, this is good," Shar exclaimed. "Okay, Raymond, everyone loves you but now you get to go join your family again. On the count of three," she shouted and looked at the crowd. "Let's start the countdown," she called to a lady on the beach, who relayed the message as Shar held up one hand with her pointer finger up. "One," she called and the crowd repeated her. "Two! Three!" And with everyone shouting the number, they tilted the tub and the sea turtle slid into the water.

Cheers went up from the crowd as the turtle swam out and then bobbed up and seemed to play in the surf, as if enjoying the attention, and then it dove and disappeared. Shar spun toward them all; elation lit her face. Jillian gave her a high five and then looked up at him and there was elation in her expression too.

"It gives me chill bumps each time we do this. I

just hope he lives safe and happy."

"Me too." He gently held her arm to assist her as they trudged back up to shore.

"Oh." She gasped and looked down at his wet running shoes. "You weren't barefoot. I don't know what I was thinking." She'd stepped out of her flip-flops prior to entering the water.

"It's fine. They wash. I wouldn't have missed that for anything."

"Thanks, buddy," Gage said, as he passed by. "I'm glad you could help out."

"Any time," Ryan said as he and Jillian moved out of the way so the ambulance could pack up and head out.

"Talk to you later, Shar," Jillian called and walked with him to the side.

Shar winked at Jillian. "Yeah, don't you dare not call me, okay?"

He saw Jillian color slightly and she didn't answer as she picked up her sandals and started to walk. His curiosity snagged, he walked beside her. "I'm going to remove my shoes. Could you wait for a minute?"

"Sure." She paused and watched him as he bent down and untied his shoestrings and tugged the now sand-encrusted shoes and socks. "Good ole sand." She laughed.

"Yeah, hang on." He picked the shoes up and jogged to the water to drench them in the water and then jogged back and stuffed the socks inside them. "Okay, ready." They walked a little way before either said anything. He felt at peace being in her presence.

"That was awesome," he said, because it was, and he suddenly had trouble finding something to say.

"Yes, always." Pride glittered in Jillian's eyes and it was clear to Ryan that what she said was so true.

"She is amazing."

"Yes. She was helping Cali and me at the resort and she was basically running herself ragged—getting up early to jog the beaches, watching for injured turtles. During the egg laying seasons, she would jog all the beaches in rotations, watching for endangered eggs, filling out paperwork for that when she would find the nest. And then she was coming to work, working with us…it was too much."

"It sounds like it."

"Helping with the resort in the PR department wasn't exactly her most enjoyable moments. She was better at it than she believed but her thing is rescuing sea turtles—organizing weddings, not so much. So Olivia came into the group and set her free." She grinned.

"That's definitely her heart. But you love what you do, so you're not looking for a way to leave."

"Oh, I love it. No leaving for me."

"I thought so. I haven't been in since I came back but I've passed by and it looks great. The landscaping is fantastic on the exterior and I hear it's even better inside due to you. Plus, I'm sure you're a wonderful host. I remember when your mom and dad always held those parties for the people staying at the resort and invited anyone who wanted to come and they loved it. I figure you're that way."

"Thank you. They had a way with people and still do. We are trying to continue the legacy that they built at the resort. We're updating it because it needs freshening up and we have to do it in order to attract small conferences and weddings and family get-togethers and things like that. But overall, we are striving to keep the same feel that Mom and Dad always managed."

"I would think that this mural is a fantastic draw." He nodded at the mural in front of them. They stopped walking to study it.

"Grant went beyond the call of duty for that masterpiece."

Ryan studied the brilliant colored coral reef that Grant had painted and the fish and the dolphins that were the focal point of the four-story piece of artwork. "Jax is very proud of the work he was able to do on this."

"He should be. He's talented. Have you heard from him since they left?"

"A couple of times but he says they keep a pretty hard schedule when they're creating."

"Yes, they do. This was done in less than a week once he started the actual painting. It's Grant getting the feel for the area and deciding what's special that he should paint that is the lengthy part, it seems."

They stood close together and Ryan had the urge to put an arm around her shoulders and to draw her in for a hug. *A kiss.* He tried not to let his imagination go there. "You stay busy. When do you fit dating into your schedule?"

"Oh, I do…um. Here and there."

Was it just him or was she hedging? His chest tightened at the thought that she didn't sound too committed. "So, your boyfriend—he doesn't mind dating here and there?"

Her long lashes nearly touched her eyebrows as her eyes widened. "Um, no."

Jillian Sinclair could not pull off a poker face if she wanted to. She was up to something. *But what? Why hedge on this with him?*

"Let's just say for the sake of it that I was dating you," he said. Her expression faltered as he lifted his hand and took a loose strand of her thick hair between his fingertips. It was as soft and silky as it looked. She swallowed hard enough that her tiny jaws tensed. He held her gaze with eyes full of serious truth. "Here and there dating you would not cut it for me."

Her lips parted and a soft, "Oh," escaped as her footing shifted in the sand.

She was so lovely. He could not help himself as he leaned forward so their faces were very close. "I would want to be at your side every moment you let me be there."

"Oh," she said again. Her breaths were little puffs against his lips.

"So true," he murmured as the world seemed to spin around him. Ryan leaned closer and covered her lips with his.

The world stopped revolving the instant her soft lips joined his. Her welcomed hand came gently to his cheek; her trembling fingertips light as butterflies against his skin caught his heart instantly. His heart thundered and he felt as if he were in heaven.

Suddenly Jillian froze and pulled back. "Oh," she gasped, her expression one of shock. "I have to go." She practically stumbled on the sand as she moved to get away from him

Shocked himself, Ryan watched her leave, fighting the need to go after her.

He hadn't meant to kiss her. Hadn't meant to cross that line. But he had and now he knew without a doubt that he was in trouble.

Big trouble, because that hadn't been just a kiss....

CHAPTER SIX

He'd kissed her.

And she kissed him back.

Jillian did not stop as she raced from the beach onto the Windswept Bay Resort property. She kept moving past the pool with another of the gorgeous murals Grant had painted. She didn't even glance at the beautiful painting as her mind reeled from what had happened.

She crossed the small white bridge over the swan lagoon and headed toward the rear entrance stairs that would lead up to the office. She had to grab the keys to her car before she could drive away and be alone, so she hoped she didn't run into her sisters.

She made it into the office and was relieved to find it empty. Her heart thundered erratically; her hands shook as she grabbed her purse and dug in it for her keys and then headed toward the stairs.

She was halfway across the lobby, headed toward the hall that would take her to the side parking lot and her car, when she heard her name.

"Jillian, what's your hurry?"

She stopped and turned to see Horace Finley, the head maintenance man, looking at her with worry on his face. Abe stood beside him.

"Are you okay?" Abe asked.

"'Cause you don't look so good," Horace commented, staring at her hard from beneath bushy brows. Horace had worked at the resort since before she was born—probably since the beginning of time. He was wonderful, competent, and took care of business. He was also blunt.

"I'm fine," she denied.

"Honey, you look like you just saw a ghost." He

scratched his head.

Abe stepped forward. "Can I help you?"

Horace looked from Abe to her and gave a small nod. "I think I will let you handle this. You need anything, young lady, you just let me know and I'll take care of it, okay? Right now I better get home to Mrs. Finley. I think she's got my supper ready."

At least he hadn't pushed. Abe, on the other hand, looked less inclined to dismiss her shell-shocked expression and walk away. Horace probably only did it because he knew that Abe was quite able to help her.

"I'm fine, Abe. I just need to go." She walked toward the hall and Abe fell into step beside her. He was broad shouldered, capable, and one she felt could handle anything. Why there was no spark between them, heaven only knew. And after what she just experienced with Ryan, she wondered whether she could ever settle for anything less than an overpowering abundance of butterflies.

Because there had been crazy, wild, overpowering butterflies.

And he had just disrupted her entire world with a

light, tender kiss. It had been so sweet. He'd taken her breath away and she still couldn't find her voice.

When they reached the end of the hall, Abe pushed the door open and held it for her. She passed between him and the door, brushing his arm as she moved past him into the sunlight. His nearness caused no flutters of anything. Not so with Ryan. The moment she'd turned to find him beside her, everything that could flutter got into motion.

And that was *before* he kissed her. She looked up at Abe.

He smiled gently. "You really do look upset, have looked and acted upset for days. At least every time I've been around you. Can I help you? Do you want to go somewhere and talk?"

"Yes, could we?" She was pushing things; she knew it. She should go home. But Abe had offered and he could be her path to the future she wanted—or would settle for. *Oh, what an awful-sounding, desperate thought.*

"My truck is over here." His deep voice rumbled softly as he leaned slightly and pointed over her shoulder toward the large crew cab at the edge of the parking lot. She nodded and let him lead the way and open the passenger door for her.

Jillian was getting inside when Grace, who managed the resort for them, got out of her car a few spaces away.

"Hi." She smiled at Jillian and then her gaze lifted to Abe. Jillian saw Grace's eyes light up. "Hello, Abe," she said, and then looked from Abe to her. "Are you going out?"

Jillian might be wrong but she thought that she heard tension in Grace's question.

"We're going for a drink." Abe smiled at Grace.

Jillian thought his voice softened. "To talk," Jillian added, quickly. "Are you working this evening?"

Grace nodded as she pulled her purse onto her shoulder and her hand tightened on her purse strap. "I am. I had to take Donovan to the doctor today for a checkup so I traded for the late shift."

Abe's head tilted. "Donovan?"

Grace brightened. "Yes, my son. He's five."

"And adorable," Jillian added. "And smarter than any five-year-old I've ever met—maybe any fifty-year-old."

"Is he okay?" Abe asked and Grace nodded.

"He is. He has a cold. He was disgusted because the doctor did not give him any medicine to help him."

Abe laughed. "My daughter would have been ecstatic."

Grace's eyes brightened. "I didn't know you had a child either."

Jillian watched them and wondered why these two weren't dating. There seemed to be something passing between them.

"Yes, my wife died a few years ago. It's been tough on her but she's starting to do better."

"I'm so sorry about your wife," Grace said. "It's hard raising kids alone. Donovan misses his dad. He walked out on us two years ago and it's been hard on him. At the moment, Donovan thinks he's smarter than me. Anyway, I need to get to work and let you two go. Sorry."

Jillian was positive Grace knew exactly what

butterflies and erratic heartbeats felt like and she was having them while talking to Abe.

"It's okay," Jillian assured her, feeling that she was the third wheel.

"If you ever need me to help in some way, let me know. Maybe he'd enjoy coming to work for a day?"

"Oh," Grace said, softly. "That's a very nice offer. I'll keep that in mind. Now I need to get to work. You two have a nice time." And then she hurried to the side entrance and was gone.

Abe watched her go. Jillian studied his profile and wondered whether he might be wishing he was assisting Grace into his truck instead of her. The thought didn't bother her at all.

"Okay, I guess we're ready." He turned back to her to see that she was settled in the seat with her seat belt already snapped in place.

Jillian chuckled, suddenly feeling lighthearted. "I think we are," she said.

Moments later, they were at a small outdoor bar that served all kinds of tropical drinks, both alcoholic and nonalcoholic, in a beautiful setting. They grabbed the table beneath a thatched umbrella. Jillian ordered a glass of strawberry lemonade. She had not had an ounce of alcohol since her prom night.

As Abe ordered the same, her thoughts went to prom night. The most humiliating night of her life. When she'd pushed boundaries and had a few drinks for the first time in her life and had reacted overwhelmingly badly. She'd been more tipsy than she had believed, thus when she had been rescued from her drunk prom date by her hero, Ryan, her inhibitions were on the loose.

She'd unleashed all of her secret hopes and dreams on him, including the fact that she loved him…and that she wanted to have his babies.

"Earth to Jillian," Abe said from across the table.

"Sorry. I have a lot on my mind."

"It seems so." He cupped his hands together on the table in the same manner that she'd cupped her own hands.

"Abe." She sighed. "You have no idea."

"I hope that you consider me a friend. Because I consider you a friend." He reached across the table, took her hand and squeezed gently. His gaze met hers. There were no sparks, no floaters—nothing except the comfort of his strong hand on hers.

"I do consider you as a friend, but I need to say something. I can't go out with you anymore. I hope you aren't hurt by that."

He took the news with a thoughtful look. "I felt like you felt that way," he said. "You and I both know there's no chemistry between us. You deserve more than that and I can tell you don't feel fireworks and explosions when I hold your hand."

"You are a wonderful man."

"Again, I hope so. My mama would be glad to know that you think that. But you and I both know that you deserve to marry a wonderful man who also drives you crazy with love. You don't need to settle for anything less than that. That's what I felt for my wife and finding that again might be more than I can ever find again. But this is about you. If telling me you are cutting me loose is what's had you so tied up in knots, then I'm glad we're getting this off the table." He sat back as their lemonades were brought and thanked the waitress.

When they were alone again, Jillian sipped her drink before she spoke. "You are a very smart man, Abe."

As it turned out, by the time Abe dropped her off at the resort to pick up her car, she hadn't shared anything else personal with him. They were friends but settling that had been a relief to her. She'd known when she'd seen him talking with Grace that she needed to move on. She hadn't been fair to him by even thinking of settling. He deserved more than that.

And so did she…but that was her problem.

CHAPTER SEVEN

Two days after being kissed by Ryan and cutting any romantic ties with Abe, Jillian was still in a state of turmoil about her life but she was relieved that she and Abe had talked. And she had been glad when she saw him and Grace talking in the lobby. They might be a great match…she hoped so.

Today she'd worn a dress and sandals because they had three small weddings going on at the resort. They'd finished the flowerbeds just in time. Her job today had been to watch over the intimate wedding in the secluded fountain area. Cali had taken on the larger one at the beach, and Olivia had taken the one in the banquet room. After the wedding, Jillian headed back to the office and was startled when she saw Ryan walking toward her across the courtyard. Her heart skipped and her day brightened instantly. He wore shorts, a surfing T-shirt, and boat shoes; his brown eyes warmed her heart as they met hers. She hadn't seen him since he kissed her and there was no use denying that she hadn't missed him. She had.

She hadn't been able to stop thinking about him.

"Hi," he said. "I needed to see you. I wondered if I could take you away from here for a little while."

Unable to stop herself, she nodded. "That will be nice, actually."

He grinned. "It's my lucky day."

"Give me a minute." She pulled out her phone and messaged Cali that the wedding had gone well and she was leaving for the day. She reminded herself that she was being reckless and would regret this. She needed to tread carefully. But she found, at the moment, all she wanted to do was spend a few moments with Ryan. It would be okay.

Within minutes, she was following him out to the parking lot to his truck. He held the door open for her.

"Your chariot awaits." She moved past him and he helped her into the seat and then leaned close. "If I wasn't afraid of running you off, I would kiss you right now."

Butterflies, butterflies, butterflies.

She must have looked startled by his words because he smiled and then stepped back and closed the door. Her mouth had gone dry as he walked around the truck to his side and slid behind the wheel. She was playing with fire and she knew it. Or was she just flying by the seat of her pants? Something that one rarely classified as a Jillian trait. *Too late to back out.*

He was in the truck quickly and they were on their way.

"I hope this isn't going to cause a problem between you and your boyfriend." He glanced at her. "I kissed you, and I wouldn't want to do that if you're serious about someone. I got the feeling you aren't serious. If I'm wrong, let me know and I'll back off."

His words sent a shiver through her. "No, there is

no boyfriend."

"The men of Windswept Bay must be blind, is all I can say."

She laughed. "You are terrible." *What would life with Ryan be like?* The question filled her mind, tickled her insides, and tightened the coil of tension inside of her.

"No—truthful, from where I sit."

She didn't know what to say to that. He drove through the streets, turned in to the Lagoon Adventures parking lot and turned off the truck. She knew she was treading in dangerous waters. She should tell him now that there were reasons why he might not want to get involved with her. She needed to tell him.

He turned in the seat and placed his arm across the back of it; he played with a strand of her hair. "I respect you, Jillian. I haven't slept the last two nights thinking about you. I cannot get you off my mind. I think you need to know my life is up in the air right now and I feel like I have no right to want to spend time with you."

Her mouth was dry. "I'm here, feeling a little

overwhelmed," she said, softly. "But I can't not be here."

He smiled. "That is what I want to hear. Now, I want to take you for a ride down this lagoon. I spend all my days watching couples enjoy this beautiful place and it is driving me crazy. I need to take you to view the waterfalls."

"I would love that." She would give in to this moment and enjoy spending time with Ryan. *And then she would tell him.*

She was repeating that mantra moments later as he led her to the back deck, where the kayaks were. A very small metal flat bottom boat with a trolling motor was tied to the dock.

"It'll get dark soon so I thought we'd take the boat to the waterfall. It's a little quicker that way. It is after hours, so we need to get down there before it gets too dark."

"Great. I haven't been on the lagoon since high school. I remember a couple of girlfriends and I had fun being followed down the lagoon by a manatee."

"Manatees like the lagoon. They're here so you'll

probably see one again. People love seeing them."

He held out a life vest for her to slip her arms into. "Safety first," he said. She slipped her arms in and he snapped her vest for her, which put him standing close to her. Jillian studied him as he clicked the safety snaps together. He smiled when he did it and for a moment she thought he was going to kiss her. But then he put his own vest on and moved to the boat and held his hand out to her.

"Ready?" he asked.

It was a loaded question. Jillian was so ready.

They rode along the lagoon, the dappled sunlight filtering in through the overhead canopy of trees. The lazy lagoon eventually released out into the ocean but the small waterfall about halfway along the trip was a favorite part of the ride. The small motorboat made the trip faster but they did see a huge manatee lumbering slowly along the canal. "We use a trolling motor on the boat so we won't hurt any of the wildlife in here. The sea turtles and manatees could be really in danger if I was speeding up and down this area with a large boat motor and didn't have time to avoid them."

"This is perfect, though—gets you here quicker if you need to help someone and keeps the animals safe too. Oh, beautiful." She gasped as they rounded the bend and she saw the waterfall. There were many waterfalls in the area, mainly because, unlike much of the flatter lands just off the coastline, Windswept Bay was actually an island and it had hills and taller peaks, unlike other places along the Florida coastline. Of course, the island's waterfalls were nothing compared to larger tropical islands in other areas. But they were still beautiful.

"I think so. I'm glad you came," Ryan said.

"Me too."

They were peaceful but most of all they added a very romantic backdrop for the island. And picnics were often a fun getaway for the tourists who came to relax, or the honeymooners wanting some special memories, and the islanders who appreciated what their island had to offer. It had been a long time since Jillian had enjoyed any of that...especially with a man. A special man.

And he was special. She couldn't believe the last

week had brought her to spending time with him. She had her own problems but she also had a strong feeling that Ryan would probably walk away from the island and return to his career, like he had done before.

"You're sure quiet up there." Ryan docked the boat, tying it off to the small dock.

"I was wondering how you're doing since you left here. I know you were still struggling with the loss of your sister and I know that your life's work focused on stopping drug dealing. But how are you doing?"

He looked thoughtful as he climbed from the boat to the dock and held a hand out to her.

"I do okay. Good. My sister didn't deserve what happened to her. She made some wrong choices that many youth from all backgrounds make. She fell victim to vultures. I've been obsessed, I think, with that and I can't let it go. My work has been…lonely in many ways, isolating in many ways, but rewarding when I help rid society of one more thug."

Jillian stared at him and her heart went out to him. He'd chosen to live through the years in undercover work and that couldn't have been easy.

He reached for the picnic basket and then led the way over to a grassy area that they kept cleared out for picnics. He spread out the blanket that was just inside the basket. Jillian took a seat in the center and crossed her legs under her, watching him as he sat down.

It didn't seem real that things she'd once dreamed of with him were happening right now. She was actually sitting here, about to have a picnic with Ryan Locke. A lump lodged in her throat…those teenaged dreams were now coming true but there was so much surrounding this moment. "When is enough?" The question came out of left field and she watched the play of emotion on his face, the hardening of his eyes as he looked off and studied the far distant image that only he could see in the trees. *Why hadn't she just enjoyed this time instead of pushing?*

"I don't know, Jillian. I don't know." He looked back at her and he smiled sadly. "I've come back here to help Jax out and I know I needed this time. My captain demanded it. I wasn't happy at first but now I'm realizing it was necessary. I think at some point you can get battle-weary. Be in the field so long, you lose perspective and my superiors are afraid that's happened to me. I may only have a desk job waiting for me when I go back. They've basically told me it's time for me to find a life. To get some perspective."

"And how do you feel about that?" Her heart had picked up speed as she watched him, listened to him and she wondered whether there was a chance that he would listen to what they were saying.

"I'm at a crossroads, like I said. I don't know what I'm going to do."

She was at a crossroads, too, and didn't know what she was going to do either.

He pulled a couple of soft drinks from the container and handed her one; it was her favorite. She wondered how he remembered such a detail considering it had been years since they'd hung out at family gatherings. She'd been a kid but he probably had always been good with remembering details. And that would come into play with being an undercover detective, or whatever he was called.

He smiled. "Yep, I remember. Once you went with me and Levi to pick up supplies for your mom and dad. We were having a Thanksgiving gathering at the resort and I remember you saying that Dr. Pepper was your favorite drink. I was unsure if it still was after all these years but I took a chance."

That answered that question. He *had* remembered that tiny detail. "You have an amazing memory."

"I'll be there, at the Thanksgiving gathering this year. I'm competing with Levi. We are going to take on Trent and Jake, and I think Max and Cam are going to compete as well."

She laughed. "Oh wow, it will be like old times. This will be fun. We'll have to throw some new kinks into the mix."

He took a drink of his Coke. "I look forward to seeing what you girls come up with."

"I doubt, even if we really wanted to, that there is anything we could really come up with that would surprise you guys."

She grew serious again. "You know, your sister would want you to live a full life. I hate that you are basically being forced out of the life that you are so dedicated to. But I'm curious as to why they're doing that. Aren't some people undercover longer than that?"

"They are. I'm on medical leave. I don't know if you knew that. I took a bullet when my cover was blown and it left me with a few problems. I also had a bad concussion and have trouble with sleep and headaches. There's a few other things that go along with it but basically I've been so deep and my cover is blown and I need to disappear to some extent. Levi and I've been talking about me coming here. I think that I can do some good here." He studied her.

Jillian froze as his words rang through her like an alarm and a bell of joy at the same time. "You would be needed here but are you safe?"

"I'm safe. I've always worn a beard and mustache when undercover. I'd be hard to recognize, even if someone from my past showed up." He busied himself pulling things out of the basket.

Jillian could have kicked herself for having started this conversation and taking them down such a serious line when they could have been enjoying the scenery and their time together. This was romantic. And she'd opened up a door into his darker side of life. But she couldn't help herself; she had to understand Ryan. Reaching out, she placed her hand on his.

"Maybe they are right. Maybe it's time for you to find a life for yourself. I get the feeling that somehow you put yourself in the same category as the…people you were trying to put behind bars."

He handed her the wrapped sandwich that he had pulled out of the basket. Immediately, he raked a hand through his hair, before he stood and walked to the water's edge.

"I do," he said. "I messed up. I made a call before my cover was blown and it was a setup. I didn't see it coming. I had let myself trust someone that I shouldn't have. I let my barriers down and I didn't see that I was being betrayed. I got too close to someone I was trying to help. She turned on me and it cost me. In my profession, if you let your guard down it can be the kiss of death. In my situation, I lived but the girl I was trying to help not only set me up—she died in the crossfire."

"Oh, Ryan."

"Yeah, it was bad. I haven't told anyone that. I

don't think I'll ever forgive myself for it. Marla was a sweet, mixed-up young woman like my sister, and I let my emotions get clouded."

Jillian stood and, unable to stop herself, she walked to Ryan and put her arms around him. "You didn't do it on purpose. I know you've saved lives during your career but you can't save them all."

He turned and looked down at her, loosely holding her in his arms as she looked up at him. "I know. But I want to."

Jillian could not stop herself; she lifted her hands and cupped his face. Her heart raced and the conviction that she was looking entirely into the eyes of a man who deeply needed to understand his worth gripped her. "You can't. But you can save some. And you can make a difference. Either way, you matter, Ryan. You matter. That means you deserve some semblance of a normal life. A happy life. You don't have to go pretend to be some bad person all the time."

His dark eyes were unmoving.

She stepped away. *How bad did he have to pretend to be while undercover? What had he seen and done? Could he acclimate to a regular life?*

"I hear you," he said, softly. "I just have to accept it."

"I believe you can because I've known you all these years. Do you know why you were the focus of all my adolescent infatuation, crushes, and total and complete adoration?"

That made him smile. "No, actually, I don't."

"My brothers are great guys and they had a lot of friends, so I was around a lot of guys growing up. But you, Ryan, were always kind to me. Always took up for me or my sisters, and I knew that I could always count on you. You can't help that I had a crush on you—you couldn't help that I threw myself at you on prom night. Being a great guy just has consequences." She cocked her head and smiled a little bit. "Yes, I'm still mortified and was so much so that it made me angry at you. That was wrong on my part, but you being a good, kind, caring man was not wrong. I'm surprised you didn't have more girls throwing themselves at you."

"No, no one but you ever did that," he said, and

she saw the teasing light return to his eyes.

Overwhelmed by everything, she turned away. Her heart thundered and her knees were weak. She knew she loved Ryan Locke.

Moving away, she sank to the blanket and looked into the picnic basket, needing something to do as her thoughts whirled. As the truth sank in. It wasn't just an adolescent crush from years ago but a real emotion for the man he'd been and the man he'd become. The devoted fighter for injustice who felt so deeply. She was stunned by the revelation. She had fallen for a good, kind, upstanding young man all those years ago. And just through his words, the deeply moving way that he felt about what he'd been through, she knew that he was still that person. A man worthy of love… *But what did that mean for her?* If he happened to fall for her, she had nothing to offer him.

Jillian closed her eyes as the reality of everything she'd feared fell on her shoulders.

CHAPTER EIGHT

The day before the Thanksgiving gathering, Jillian and her sisters were busy with the last details. She had been tremendously busy since her lagoon date with Ryan. No one seemed to notice that she was preoccupied at times and that was a good thing. Shar was busy at the sea turtle hospital; Cali had Grant home again and was preoccupied herself. And Olivia and BJ were starting to think about when they were going to try to fit in their wedding plans. So everyone was tied up with their personal lives while also keeping the resort going and planning for Thanksgiving. No one noticed Jillian's withdrawal. Even Blair seemed preoccupied since Jax had come home and so there was no intrusion from her friend either. Jillian, though, as preoccupied as she was with her worries about what to do about Ryan and having babies, noticed that Blair was not herself. She was a nervous wreck. And Jillian wondered what was going on.

She might have to ask…but really, it was not her business.

Today, everyone was on the sand, in full prep mode.

Jillian and her sisters were helping set up the children's festival area with games and activities. Her mind kept wandering back to Blair, who'd called in sick today.

"Oh, that looks so cute," Olivia exclaimed as she stood back from the banner that Max and BJ had just erected for them.

"It is," she agreed as she took in the cute picture of two turkeys inviting the children to enter the festival area. The resort was a hub of activity and her entire family was involved in getting the Thanksgiving Beach

Celebration going. There would be a large turnout. Many of the visitors of the resort were people who'd been to the island for Thanksgiving before and returned again just to be involved with the event.

Jillian concentrated on creating a festival that would bring smiles to all who came and ate lunch with them on the beach. She did not concentrate on wondering about Ryan. He had been busy also since they'd gone down to the lagoon and hadn't called or come by.

The last part of their date had been good but…stilted. She knew on her part that it was her being overwhelmed by realizing she loved him and what that meant for her. But she wasn't sure why he'd gotten quieter. *Had she gotten him to open up too much about his problems?*

Cali stopped where she was setting up a station of apple bobbing. "This is going to be a fantastic celebration this year. I know the community is excited. And I'm so glad Mom and Dad started this when we were kids."

"Me too," Shar called from where she was helping

her coworkers from the sea turtle hospital set up portable aquariums that would house some of the permanent resident turtles for everyone to see. "And we are so excited about adding the sea turtle awareness section for the kids. They are going to love this."

Jillian agreed. "You had a great idea to bring the turtles here. It adds another layer to this wonderful event."

"I can't wait to have a child of my own to celebrate this with." Cali beamed. "I'm so ready—" She paled and her gaze met Jillian's. "I mean—"

Jillian realized she was worried about mentioning babies because of her. "It's okay, Cali. I'm hoping you have a baby soon too. I'm ready to at least be an aunt. Do not feel bad that you want to be a mother. Not because of me."

"I know, but I can't help but hurt for you over this—"

"Thank you, but please don't. So are you wanting a baby soon?"

"Jillian," Shar called. "You are one sugar-coated sweet sister. And we aren't giving up on this for you."

"Me either," she said.

"Gage can't wait to have babies. So Cali is going to have to hurry to beat us. But really, who knows who will be first?"

"We are trying." Cali smiled. "But so far, it's not happened. Maybe we can have a baby before next Thanksgiving, though."

"Mom will be thrilled when she finally gets a grandchild." Jillian tried to smile. Despite what she'd just told them, she had to ignore the reminder that she might never carry a child but she was determined that she was going to focus on the blessing of adoption.

"Jillian, come over here please," Trent called from where he and Jake were constructing a climbing wall. Both her brothers had their shirts off as they worked and had gathered quite a gallery of females standing around, watching their progress. Her brothers were all in shape and trained heavily because of their military years.

"Oops, I'll be right back," she said, relieved to leave the conversation. "You gals carry on."

Trudging through the sand, she reached Trent.

"What can I do for you?" she asked.

"Did you say you were going to add something here?" He made circular motions with his hands, which flexed his muscles, and she heard a few oohs and ahhs from the admiring public. Trent shot a grin in their direction.

"Yes, plants. I want to add greenery around the base of these barriers to give you guys something more to jump over. It'll make it more exciting for your fans to watch."

Max looked dubious. "What fans?"

"Ha, you know who I'm talking about."

Trent grinned. "It's tough, you know."

"Sure, I know—it's a hardship." She laughed, remembering a time when she used to be the one standing off to the side, listening to all of her friends and all the older girls admiring her older brothers while she secretly admired Ryan.

"I've got them lined up over there." She pointed toward an area where supplies were stacked. There was a line of potted shrubs. "Just plant the pots in the sand and we'll pull them out on Friday. It's simply for looks."

"Hardship, you mean," Max corrected her.

"Oh, right. Extra work for you boys. And the water trench is going to be fun. All for a good cause. You men raise a lot of money every year and don't you forget it."

First responders, military, firemen, police: they loved the competition of the obstacle course challenge. It was for a great cause, as the entry fee and the donations that were taken up during the day went to the local food banks.

"Spectators are going to be busy either admiring our battles with each other or laughing at the fools we make of each other." Trent chuckled.

Max grinned. "There have been a few battles going on in the water trenches at times over the years."

"I doubt that'll change," Ryan said from behind Jillian.

She turned to find Ryan approaching, carrying a tarp. Her pulse danced.

He looked at her. "Speaking of a trench, we've come to build a water trench just for the purpose of battling it out." Ryan smiled at her. "Levi couldn't make it. He got called out, so he asked me if I could run this over to you. I've been off all day. Jax is handling the Lagoon since he's back in town."

"Sure." She led the way over to the stakes that marked where the water pit would be. "Thanks for bringing that over." She felt awkward. Not that she was sure what she needed to do or wanted from all of this.

"I was glad to do it," he said. "How you doing? I've been thinking about you."

"I hope it was a good day off. I've had you on my mind too," she said, unable to deny the truth.

"It's looking good." He looked around. "It looks busy. You want this in the obstacle course?"

"Sure." She was aware that her brothers were staring and her sisters were too. The girls knew there was something going on but did her brothers suspect something was brewing between her and Ryan?

He smiled at her as she walked beside him toward the stakes. "I've been thinking about what we talked about the other day. I actually slept two nights in a row a little better than I have in a long time."

They stopped beside the stake. Butterflies were multiplying at the rate of bunnies inside Jillian's chest. "I'm glad for you. Really, I am. You have decisions to make and I hope that maybe I can help in some way."

"You have. Now, how do you want this pit done? It's been a few years since I was here for the obstacle course. I better grab a shovel too."

"Yes, I think you need to get a shovel and grab some of my brothers to help you because there's no sense you doing this all by yourself. Besides, it would give all those spectators more to watch. If you rip your shirt off like Trent and Max, you'll probably grow the crowd more."

"Long as it grew by one, that'd be fine with me. Would you be in that group?"

She laughed. "I have much more to do than stand around watching a bunch of guys flex their muscles in the sunshine."

"Well, that's a little disappointing." He laughed and they headed over toward the rest of the group.

"Okay, big guys," she called to all her brothers. "I

know that you're thinking that I was going to have Ryan here dig that pit by himself, but it's not happening. You all know where the shovels are." She turned toward the swimsuit-clad women. "Come back tomorrow for Thanksgiving lunch. Everyone is invited and this obstacle course is a yearly highlight. Donations go to help our community. They'll be battling it out on the course. It's always fun to watch. What do you think of that?"

Clapping erupted as well as a few whistles and cheers; Jillian winked at her brothers and Ryan. "There you go, guys. Now get to work."

Ryan shot her a grunt. "Gee, thanks."

"You're very welcome. Remember, it's for a good cause." She laughed and headed back to the kids' area. She was going to have to concentrate on not becoming one of the adoring fan girls watching him.

But, a peek every now and again might be okay.

Cali, Olivia, and Shar all watched her as she walked their way.

"So," Cali said. "That's the way it is."

"Uh-huh." Shar grinned. "I don't even think she

needs to say anything. It's written on her face."

Olivia just smiled. "I think tomorrow and the next few weeks are going to be fun to watch and see what happens to our Jillian, the quiet one."

Jillian felt her cheeks heat in a blush. "I'm in trouble. I haven't told him anything. He might leave."

Shar put her hand on her hip and cocked her head. "And he might stay too."

And that was the problem. She had to tell him.

Jillian was too busy, a very good thing, to think about anything but the Thanksgiving Day lunch and festivities. She had to put her personal life on hold—all of it—to deal with the day. The night had been pretty sleepless but she'd managed a few hours and had arrived early to help in the kitchen and anywhere else she might need to lend a hand.

The chefs at the resort had prepared so much turkey and assortments of delicious dishes and would keep them coming as needed. The resort charged a nominal fee for lunch to cover expenses but made sure that anyone who wanted to come was able to. No one had to spend Thanksgiving alone unless they just wanted to. That was her parents' reasoning for starting the tradition and they were here today, carrying it on.

People came from all over and the ticket sales had been brisk; the resort itself was booked. The small kids' festival had been added when Jillian and her brothers and sisters were young and was an attraction all by itself. Families had built traditions around attending year after year.

When Ryan showed up, Jillian was visiting with a couple of older women who were widows and had been booking a night in the resort for years. Patsy and Francine were lively and had taken a special liking to Jillian on their first visit about four years ago. Probably because she'd sat down and ate with them.

Francine was in her eighties and was still an avid golfer who loved to tease. She nudged Jillian's arm as Ryan came through the crowd and headed toward them.

"Now that is one handsome young man. Oh, Jilly, he's coming this way—act normal," she said, using the name they'd started calling Jillian years ago.

"How else am I going to act?" Of course, her blood pressure had spiked but there was no way she was letting Francine or Patsy know that.

"Oh," Patsy muttered under her breath as she pushed her glasses closer to her eyes. "He is one foxy man."

"Hush, Patsy. They don't use that term anymore. He's a hunk."

The younger woman, by a decade, frowned. "Well, I use it. He's a fox. Do you know him, Jilly? He has his eye on you."

"Like a heat-seeking missile," Francine added and rammed her arm again when Jillian didn't answer.

"Yes, I know him."

"Well, this should be interesting," Patsy said.

His eyes were sparkling and his smile reached them. "Hi," he said to her and then smiled at her friends. "I'm Ryan. I don't believe we've met."

"Francine, and this is Patsy," Francine said.

"Are you competing?" Patsy asked.

Francine leaned close to Jillian and muttered, "I

hope so."

Ryan couldn't help but hear and he chuckled. "I am. First time in a long time. It will be fun."

"I didn't think I ever saw you before." Patsy shot a coy glance at Jillian. "So you know our Jilly?"

"She's the best," Francine stated.

"Yes, we've known each other for a long time."

"Really? Then what's your holdup?" Patsy demanded.

"Excuse me?" he said and Jillian suddenly felt very uncomfortable. As if she sensed a bad case of flu coming on or something equally terrible.

"You like her," Francine snapped.

Ryan's eyes met Jillian's. "Yes, ma'am, I do."

Patsy rammed her glasses closer to her eyes since they'd slid down again. "Yes, those eyes don't lie. So why haven't you made an honest woman out of her?"

Jillian gasped. "Girls, we're not—"

"Why not?" Francine cut her off.

Jillian sputtered. "I, he…okay, hold on," she warned, getting her feet back under her. "You two mischief makers need to go grab some turkey."

Ryan was grinning and she could tell he was holding back laughter.

Francine gave him an up-and-down look. "We'll do that. But, remember, cutie-patootie, we saw the look."

"Time is wasting. We both know," Patsy said. "We've had sweet love and lost it. But we remember."

And with that, they walked off.

"You have fun friends," Ryan said. "Do they try and match you up often?"

Jillian bit her lip. "Actually, no. That was the first time."

"Oh," he said. "Well—"

"They are huge teasers. Bad teasers. But they do know a good man when they see him. I'm glad you're here. It's a great turnout."

"Yeah, it is. Sorry I'm running a little late."

She chuckled. "If you had arrived earlier, you may have been harassed more. Eating is just getting started, so go say hi to Mom and Dad—they'll want to see you again. And then grab a plate. You'll want to eat soon before the challenge starts."

He nodded and looked around. "Wow, Jillian, there are a lot of people here. This is unbelievable. And look at your parents. They are beaming and completely in their element."

"Yeah, this is their vision working." Her eyes welled with tears of pride. "It shows what a small idea can do. Seeing it makes me happy."

Ryan was studying her. "Of course it does. It suits you too."

It did. "It makes my heart happy."

"I'm glad I get to be a part of it this year." He sobered and glanced around, watching kids running around, laughing. "I spent many Thanksgiving Days here while Dad was working. I'm very grateful and very, very thankful to be a part of this."

"I'm glad you are too. Where is your dad today? Is he still fishing?"

"Yes. Called and said he had another group to take out. He loves it. I'm glad he's enjoying himself. That's what retirement is for."

She eyed him. "Says the man who doesn't know when to quit."

His expression clouded. "Right. But, I'm a fast learner."

"Oh really?"

He nodded and he leaned close. "When I really want something, I make changes."

A shiver raced over Jillian and her breath caught just as he smiled and then he walked off.

Her heart squeezed so hard it hurt.

She wanted good for Ryan so much. She wanted him to be free of the false belief that she feared he carried that he didn't deserve to feel simple pleasures.

She was still walking around, greeting people, when Ryan returned a few minutes later and took her arm.

"Let's go get you something to eat." He took her hand and held tight. Her stomach felt bottomless as he gently tugged her toward the food. "You have worked your tootsie off and deserve to eat, too, you know."

Ryan continued to hold her hand as they walked to the tables of food; after they got their plates filled, he led the way to the table and they squeezed in among her brothers and sisters.

Blair looked a little pale but she was smiling and Jax was smiling too.

"I want to announce something." He looked at Ryan and then everyone. "I just asked Blair to marry me."

Congratulations erupted from everyone. Jillian scooted her chair out and went to hug Blair.

"I am so excited for you. I knew he would ask you soon."

Ryan came and hugged her too and clapped Jax on the shoulder. "This is awesome."

"Thanks all of you," Jax said. "I've been ready for this step for the longest time. And now she said yes. I'm the luckiest man alive. And there is more. We're going to have a baby."

Congratulations started again. And Jillian hugged Blair once more, suddenly understanding her friend's missing work a few days and being quiet those last days before Jax came home. She'd been worried.

Blair had tears in her eyes. "I just learned last

week and I've been so worried," she said softly to Jillian. "But Jax is so happy. And he asked me immediately to marry him."

"No worries for you two. This baby will know it has two parents who love him or her."

Blair nodded and her hand went to her stomach. "Yes. With all our hearts."

The doctor's words rang through Jillian as if it were that first morning. "*Your opportunities for conceiving will diminish substantially in the next couple of years. For your best chance, now would be the time.*"

Later, telling herself she was happy for Blair and not jealous…maybe wishful, Jillian went to take up her post at the kiddie festival. She took up her station at the apple bobbing and waited for the little kids to come try their luck bobbing for a bright, shiny apple. Thankfully there were so many kids that she was blissfully unable to concentrate on her own troubles while she helped them have a good time. And then

Ryan strode up, grinning and reminding her all the more what she wanted and was afraid to ask for. To hope for. To dream of.

"You need some help?" he asked.

"Sure," she said, trying hard for a smile.

Before she could say more, the little boy who'd been studying the apples looked up at Ryan and grinned. He was missing a tooth in front and he had freckles across his cheeks; he looked to be about four. His mother stood off to the side with her camera and was waiting to take his picture whenever he finally decided to put his head in the water and bob for the apple.

"Hey, mister, do you know how to do this?" He squinted at Ryan.

Ryan chuckled. "It's been a long time since I did it, but I can sure try. Do you need me to show you?"

The little kid nodded. "Please." The glee and excitement was evident in the boy's tone and his wide eyes.

Ryan didn't hesitate as he knelt in the sand and held up his hand. "Give me five," he said.

Instantly, the boy slapped Ryan's hand with his tiny one and exclaimed, "You can do it!"

Ryan laughed. "What's your name?"

"Kevin Donald Price," the little boy stated proudly.

"Kevin Donald Price—that is a big name for a little boy." Ryan grinned and Kevin beamed.

"You can just call me Kevin. All my friends do."

"Well, Kevin, here goes." Ryan grabbed the edge of the metal washtub holding the three plump red apples; then he winked at Kevin and dunked his entire head in the tub.

Kevin, so small, laughed and jumped ecstatically. His excitement was contagious and other kids gathered around as Ryan pulled his dripping head out of the water and shook it hard, like a wet dog would do. Water went everywhere, getting the boy and anyone in his path wet. Squeals of delight erupted from the kids.

Then Ryan looked confused. "Did I miss the apple?"

More giggles. Kevin pointed. "Yes, you missed the whole thing."

"But you can try again," a little girl stepped up and told him.

Not to be outdone, Kevin moved closer. "Yes, you can. My mom says we should never give up."

"She's right," Ryan agreed.

Jillian melted at the sweetness of Ryan's expression and treatment of the little boy and the other children. Her heart sighed. *Ryan would make a great dad.*

More kids came over and watched as he acted silly a few more times as the kids tried hard to help him figure out how to get the apple with his teeth. Finally, just when they thought he would never learn, he grabbed an apple and rose up, holding it in his teeth.

The kids loved it and were clapping and jumping. Jillian laughed watching them and felt so drawn to Ryan in that moment, she almost threw her arms around his neck and told him she loved him. *Been there, done that.* Thankfully she restrained her excitement and stayed where she was.

He raked a hand through his wet hair and grinned at the kids. "Okay, it's time for you rugrats to try your hand at it. And I hope you can do better than me."

He'd made it possible for the worst child apple bobber to be better than he was. The kids were all able to bite the apple by at least their sixth try. Ryan stayed and cheered each child on. Before the kids left, they knew him by name and he knew them by name.

There was excitement coming from the dunking booth farther down the row of events and she saw Jake on the seat as Trent prepared to throw a baseball at the bull's-eye.

Her brothers had a crowd gathered around, too; it just happened to be females instead of children. And although Ryan could easily have been down there competing with her brothers, he'd chosen dunking for apples with the kids. He was perfect that way.

CHAPTER NINE

Moments later, the call for obstacle course participators to come to the starting line was announced over the bullhorn by her dad.

"That's me," Ryan said. "Are you going to root for me, Jillian?"

"Of course."

"Then I'll win."

She looked wary. "Are you up to that challenge? Aren't you still healing?"

"I'm well enough. See you at the finish line."

She watched him walk away; her love swelled

inside her and made her heart ache.

A few moments later, standing on the sidelines, everyone cheered as the men lined up. Levi and Ryan were attached together by rope around their waist, like each of the other teams were attached. It was to hinder them and make the challenge more entertaining.

Her dad waved the flag for the race to begin and the men moved into action. Cheers erupted as the guys raced toward the first obstacle, where they had to crawl beneath a military-style rope canopy. Levi made it to the ropes one step ahead of Ryan, and he dropped to his knees, which immediately yanked Ryan down beside him. Not prepared, Ryan hit the ground on his stomach and immediately started to laugh.

"Levi, man, give me a break. You're killing me." He laughed harder and started to crawl because Levi wasn't letting up as he led the way.

Jillian started to laugh too, finding joy in watching Ryan relax and enjoy himself so much.

By the time they made it to the end of the first obstacle, Trent and Max had passed them up and several other teams—including Jake and Gage, Cam and Grant, and BJ and Jax—were hanging close. They made it to the wall; being attached by a rope made it a really hard challenge because they had to time their approach together. Ryan and Levi had been partners for years before Ryan moved away and their past success came into play as they reached the wall, counted a quick *one, two, three* and jumped to grab the top ledge. They made it, kicked their legs over and rolled over the wall together ahead of everyone else.

And one after the other, the teams made it over and charged after Levi and Ryan. Trent and Max weren't giving up the lead easy and plowed into the trench at a close second.

Levi and Ryan moved through every other obstacle in unison, working in teamwork like no others were able to do. It was more than obvious that they made a perfect team.

They made it to the tire run. Ryan and Levi blasted through it like they had when they'd been the last two legs of the championship mile relay team.

She spotted little Kevin cheering hard for Ryan. And when they reached the last obstacle, crawling on their stomachs through the watered-down sandpit, they were neck and neck with Max and Trent. Kevin raced to the side of the pit and yelled, "Go, Ryan! Go, go, go! Never quit."

Ryan heard him and glanced over his shoulder at the kid. He grinned; he put his head down and pulled ahead of everyone. Levi kept up and they came out of the sandpit and raced to the finish line. Everyone was cheering; Kevin raced from the crowd and grabbed Ryan around the legs in a bear hug. Ryan instantly picked him up and put him on his shoulders.

Yes. She loved him.

Loved him so much she was going to burst.

All the guys were slapping high fives, including her new brothers-in-law and soon-to-be brother-in-law. Though they'd never participated in the challenge, Grant, BJ, and Gage had paired up with her brothers and done well. Cali, Olivia, and Shar raced to embrace their men and console them for their loss with kisses. She moved slowly toward Ryan. Holding in her unnaturally strong need that she'd seemed to have most of her life to throw herself at him, she restrained her enthusiasm.

"Hey, Kevin, I'm going to let you go back to your mom now. But you come by the lagoon and see me, okay?"

Kevin agreed and raced to tell his mom. Ryan immediately grabbed Jillian around the waist and pulled her close and kissed her.

His warm lips moved over hers…and oh, what a kiss it was. Right there in the middle of the crowd.

Jillian melted against him, captivated by the emotions that coursed through her. She was breathless when he released her.

"I forgot how fun that competition is. This whole day is amazing and, Jillian, you're amazing." And then he took her hand and pulled her with him from the crowd and down the path, out toward the water.

She wasn't sure what they were doing but she went anyway. It was quieter here away from all the festivities.

"I want you alone for a few minutes," he said. And when they made it to the water's edge, he grinned. "Give me just a minute, okay?" He turned toward the water and then turned back. "Don't go anywhere. I'm just rinsing off the sand." Then he laughed and jogged into the surf and dove into the water.

Jillian couldn't have moved if she'd wanted to. He surfaced, smiling like a lighthouse, and then headed back her way. He jogged out of the water and didn't hesitate as he took her hands in his.

"Jillian, I'm taking the job with Levi, and you are a huge part of the reason. I wanted to be near you. I want to…" He paused and took her face into his hands, similar to the way she'd done his face the moments they'd spent at the waterfall. She had stopped breathing the moment he'd told her he was taking the job with Levi. Now her knees turned to Jell-O.

"I want you. I love you, sweet girl. And I can't live another moment without telling you."

She froze, her heart nearly bursting with elation. These were the words she'd longed to hear most of her life. Staring into his eyes, so sincere and mesmerizingly convincing, Jillian smiled and started to speak. "I…I—" *Love you too and want you more than life itself,* her heart shouted. But the words caught in her throat. *How had she let this happen?*

She'd known he needed to know about her lack of promise where children were concerned. He deserved to know before falling in love with her. But she'd never really believed in her heart of hearts that he would fall in love with her. Or that he'd stay in Windswept Bay. And now he was telling her he'd chosen her over everything else.

"I can't believe I've done this," she said barely above a whisper as she pulled back.

His eyes clouded. "Done what?"

Her hand shook as she pushed hair from her face. The breeze lifted long strands and sent them streaming across her face. *How did she state her problem?* "I should have told you but I never thought you would ever say these words…never."

"Say what?" he urged, confusion clear in his expression.

"That you love me. I may not be able to have children, Ryan. And you deserve children. I'm sorry. I can't…do this. It's not fair…not right." She started to walk away; confusion and tears filled her own heart and blurred her eyes. *What had she been thinking?*

She hadn't been.

"Wait." Ryan moved in front of her to block her path. "You can't say that and walk away." He took her arms and held her in place. "What do you mean, you might not be able to have children?"

"I have issues," she blurted and then started to ramble. "Every day that passes is one less day that makes it possible for me to carry a child of my own. I can't ask any man to love me, or marry me knowing I'm—"

"Wait, hold on. Don't go so fast. It's okay—it's going to be okay. Now inhale, slowly…yes, there you go," he encouraged as she struggled to do as he asked.

"You've only been home barely two weeks. You can't make a statement like that out of the blue, so quickly. It's just not possible."

"It is possible. Your mother told me all of your sisters had fallen in love quickly. But this has nothing to do with them…this is what I feel for you, Jillian. And I'm concerned for you. Are you okay? Are you at risk?"

"I'm fine. I just have some problems that make my being able to get pregnant hard…and every day makes it less likely to happen. I need to try soon and even then there is no guarantee that it will happen."

How could she have ever for even a brief moment entertained the idea of finding a man and marrying quickly so that she could do this…it was too selfish.

"Marry me, Jillian. Marry me now."

She pulled away from him. "That isn't fair."

"To who?"

"To you, for one. Or to me. You can't offer me something like that on a whim and tempt me…"

"It's not a whim."

"It is."

He stared at her. "Tell me you don't love me."

"I don't love you." She forced every emotion from her expression and her voice.

"You have always been a terrible liar and you still are."

"And that is a very smug viewpoint on your part." She tried her hardest to look convincing as a smile bloomed across his precious face. "Stop smiling. This is very important, Ryan."

"Very important indeed." He took a strand of her hair between his fingers. "I love the feel of your silky hair between my fingertips." His voice was husky as he stepped close. "I love the feel of your lips against mine. And I long to feel your body against mine. But most of all, I long to know you're going to be beside me from this day forward. You say this is sudden. I say I knew you held a special place in my heart for forever. My sister's death changed the trajectory of my life. But now, it's back where it once was and that's life with you as my priority. I love you, Jillian, and my only worry about children is how that hurts you. Tell me you love me, that you'll marry me, and let's set the date."

She needed a man, and the one she loved was perfect…but it wasn't. "No, Ryan." She shook her head. "I can't. I need to get back to the celebration and help clean up."

"Jillian, you're not going to just walk away, are

you?"

She paused, turned back to him and hardened her heart to any emotion…that would come later. "Yes, I am. Marriage and children are the two most important decisions a person can make and…" She paused again. "I'm not going to let you make a mistake, because you're the guy who would sacrifice the next chapter in your life to make mine right." And he would because that was who he was—and she needed to remember that.

Ryan felt as though he'd been kicked by one of Cam's prized bulls as he watched Jillian walk away from him. This was best, giving her time to process the last few minutes and giving him time to process it too.

It had been clear to him that she'd meant what she said when she left him. And he'd be lying if he said her revelation hadn't knocked the wind out of him. Jillian deserved to have children. She was made to be a mother.

But life wasn't fair and he of all people understood that. Jen and Marla hadn't deserved to die either. But they had.

Thanksgiving was over for him. He angled across the sand away from the celebration and took the long way around to his truck. He needed time to think.

He just needed time.

CHAPTER TEN

Jillian had held herself together after she'd walked away from Ryan. It had been hard but she'd managed to help with the cleanup, though they had a great staff, who had everything under control.

When she'd finally walked into her house, she'd had all the control she could manage and the tears had come. She sat on her deck, surrounded by her flowers, but the peace she normally felt in her garden was not there.

Ryan had asked her to marry him. It was exactly what she'd wanted and what she needed for all of her dreams to come true. But she hadn't been able to go through with it.

She dabbed at her eyes and fought hard to stop the flow of tears.

The click of her garden gate opening had her looking up.

"Jillian, are you back here?" Shar called as she walked past the pink philodendrons. Olivia and Cali were with her.

"There you are," Olivia said, looking concerned.

Cali hurried forward. "We knocked but you didn't answer. Oh, Jillian, we thought you were upset when you left the resort."

And she'd thought she'd hidden it so well. She sniffed. "I'm fine."

"We are not blind," Shar snapped. "So stop with that nonsense. We love you and want to help."

Superwoman to the rescue, Jillian thought, looking at her dark-haired sister, who was giving her a sharp glare loaded with concern.

Olivia gave Shar a back-off glare and then knelt in front of Jillian. "She's just concerned for you. We all are. We saw you kissing Ryan, and we were so excited. The two of you were having so much fun all day and then you went to the beach with him."

"And came back without him." Cali sat on the edge of the chair beside Jillian.

Shar remained standing. "What on earth happened? Did you tell him you needed him to father a baby for you?"

It was Jillian's turn to glare at Shar. "I—" was all she could say and then she teared up again.

"You did." Shar gasped and Cali and Olivia did too. "You really got up the nerve and asked him? I can't believe it."

Jillian sniffed. "Well, I did." She sniffed harder and fought not to cry again but the tears rolled out of her eyes.

"And he turned you down," Cali said. "You were right—it is a hard situation to put a man in. I'm so sorry, honey."

"Come on, don't cry," Shar said, tearing up too.

"He didn't say no," she whispered. "He told me he loved me and then I told him I might not be able to have a baby and if I could, it needed to happen quick. And almost before I could get the words out, he asked me to marry him. He is the most wonderful man."

"Okay, so we should be celebrating."

"I told him no."

"You what?" Shar asked. "But you love him. You said you did."

She nodded. "And that's why I said no. I can't do it."

All of her sisters' expressions were stunned.

"No, I guess you couldn't say yes." Cali took her hand. "You wouldn't be able to let yourself do that."

Jillian dried her eyes. "I couldn't. He offered. He said he loved me and that it wasn't too quick. He said all the right things…but I want him to have everything he deserves. I could never live with myself if I married him and then couldn't give him a baby."

"But, honey, you can adopt," Olivia said.

"That's right," Shar agreed. "So I just don't get this. Marry the man, for crying out loud."

Exasperation had Jillian pushing out of the chair to separate herself from her sisters. "This is complicated.

Don't lecture me, Shar. I love you but I can't marry him and then fear that he may have regrets one day."

Shar crossed her arms and Jillian could tell she had more to say but she held it in. "It's your life," was all she said.

"So that's it." Cali looked conflicted too.

"Yes. I've had my cry and I'm going to be okay. I have options. They just don't include a man."

Olivia frowned. "I don't like it."

Jillian smiled, and knew they couldn't understand. She didn't totally. She just knew that saying yes to Ryan's proposal just wasn't right for her. "It'll be okay. I'll be okay."

She hoped...

"So when do I start?"

Levi looked up from his desk the next morning as Ryan entered the office and sprawled in the empty chair across the desk from him.

"If this means you're taking me up on my offer, then you can start yesterday." Levi stood, reached across the table and held out his hand. "I am so glad to have you on board."

Ryan leaned forward and took his friend's firm grasp. "I'm glad to be on board too. So, really, when do I start?"

Levi sank back into his chair and studied him with speculation. "You, my friend, look terrible. What's going on?"

"I'm here for the job, Levi. Not for reports on my looks."

"Grumpy *and* terrible-looking. Where did you go yesterday? I saw you and my sister walk off and you never showed back up. Is something wrong between you two?"

"What makes you think there is something between us? Because I also don't need my boss dipping into my personal life."

Levi's eyes narrowed. "For your information, I make it my business to know what's going on and I've got informants all over the place. Did you have fun floating the lagoon after hours? You think I don't know you've got a thing for Jillian? And you did kiss her yesterday. Or did you forget that?"

He should have known Levi would have his fingers tapped into everything. And he had kissed Jillian right out in front of everyone in the heat of the moment. He'd known during the apple bobbing that he loved Jillian. It had been so simple. It was as if when he'd looked up from that tub with water dripping down his face and saw the pure delight on her face, everything clicked in his heart. Stunned, he'd joined Levi in the obstacle course and everything had become clear to him as they'd fought their way to the finish line.

"So, do you have a problem with it?" He needed to be here and contribute to the town he'd always loved with the woman he had realized he loved. He just had to get her to admit she loved him. *Had he rushed her?*

"I know you, Ryan. You're a good man. But it comes down to what Jillian wants."

Ryan leaned forward, his elbows on his knees and his hands clasped. "I wish you'd told me she was having such a serious problem. Not knowing if she'll be able to conceive a baby has to be killing—"

"*Jillian can't have a baby?*" Levi's eagle eyes slammed him. "What are you talking about?"

Ryan slapped his forehead. "You didn't know?" He groaned.

"No, I didn't." Levi leaned back in his chair, devastation etched on his face, just as it was in Ryan's heart. "Jillian has always wanted children. This must be killing her."

"Yeah, but she didn't accept my offer of help—"

"Your *what*?" Levi growled. "At a time like this, she doesn't need a proposition—"

"I did not proposition your sister. I proposed."

Levi's eyes flared. "You *what*?"

"Have you not been listening to me?" Ryan stood. "I told you I love Jillian."

"You didn't say anything about love. You kissed her and I assumed there was something happening between you but you didn't say you loved her."

"Well, I do." Ryan paced the small office and then paused. "But she thinks I asked her to marry me just to help her have a baby. That's just not true."

Levi moved to the coffee pot. "How about a cup of coffee?" He poured a cup and held it out to Ryan even though he hadn't said he wanted any.

Ryan took it. "How am I going to fix this?"

His longtime friend poured himself a cup of coffee and took a cautious drink. "With time. And the old-fashioned way. You pursue her until she tells you to get lost or until she agrees to marry you."

"But that's just it—she says every day that passes limits her chances of being able to have a baby. Time isn't on her side."

"And she is well aware of that. You know Jillian—she is cautious and patient. She might think about jumping into marriage for the sake of a child but I seriously doubt she could go through with it."

He knew it was true. "So where does that leave me?"

"It leaves you with time to get your business reorganized and get settled back here for good. If Jillian loves you, she'll come around. It's Friday. You'll start here on Wednesday. Does that give you time enough to take care of everything and get back here?"

"Yeah. Jax is back and I hate to tell him but I'm not his man for running the lagoon business. I'm a cop."

Levi nodded. "Yes, you are. I didn't ever think that gig was going to go over for you. Now get your life in order and get back here. Your hometown needs you."

That was good to know. But as Ryan left the building, he wondered whether Jillian did.

CHAPTER ELEVEN

The two weeks after Thanksgiving were blessedly busy at the resort, with Christmas coming and three weddings on the beach booked, and one larger, formal wedding booked for the inside ballroom. It had them all busy and gave Jillian less time to think about herself and to do her job. Not only did she have to help organize, she was in charge of the flowers. Blair was her right-hand woman on these projects and indispensable.

Especially for the formal wedding, which required more attention on the ballroom because it lacked the view of the outside. Jillian loved bringing the ideas of the brides to life, though, and she threw herself into the wedding. She and Blair had already met earlier in the week with the bride and her mother but were meeting again today.

"I've never seen a bride more nervous than Darlene," Blair whispered to Jillian.

"She's going to get an ulcer," Jillian said sympathetically as she watched the mother and bride at the opposite end of the room having a hushed discussion. Jillian had a feeling the mother was trying to get her daughter to make up her mind. They'd had the flowers decided on and then they'd come to discuss a few changes, which had turned into a major change and then moved on into a complete third choice. She was going to give Jillian an ulcer.

"This is supposed to be a happy time," Blair continued.

"Yes, it is." Jillian thought of Ryan. She tried not to think of him too often. She knew that he'd taken the job with Levi and that he was around but she'd just run into him once at the grocery store. But, he'd asked how she was doing and she'd said she was doing good. And then they'd left. There had been no invitation to eat ice cream with him.

"I mean, I'm nervous," Blair said, breaking into Jillian's thoughts. "You know, with the baby added into the mix, I had a few reservations about how Jax was going to take the news. I worried about him feeling trapped. But he was wonderful and so happy."

"Did you agree on a date?"

"Not yet. It's taking a little juggling with family." She glanced to see whether the clients were still talking and they were. "I want to ask you if you'd be my maid of honor?"

Jillian was speechless. "Of course I will. I'd be honored."

A beautiful smile grew across Blair's face. "I hoped you would agree. I'll let you know the minute we decide on a date."

"I'll be excited," she said, just as the bride stomped toward her with her mother trailing. Jillian smiled. "So did you decide?"

"My mother thinks I'm being ridiculous," she said

dramatically. "But this is the most important day of my life. Do you get that?"

Jillian stiffened, but remained calm. "Yes, I do. What can I do to help you?"

"This room needs more. It's—"

The mother rubbed her temple. "Darlene, stop. This place will be beautiful. Jillian and her team will make certain of it. Won't you?"

"Yes." Jillian had shown her their portfolios and gone over this so many times.

"I am not looking for beautiful. I want amazing. Spectacular. And I just don't think it's there yet and we are running out of time." And then she burst into hysterical tears and stormed from the building.

"I'm so sorry," the mother apologized. "This wedding is going to kill me. It absolutely is. Please continue on with the plans and if you can make it…er, spectacular…then please do so. Money is no problem."

"I think we have our first Bridezilla." Blair sighed. "Wow."

Jillian nodded. "It appears we do. Well," she turned to Blair, "none of that for your wedding."

Blair laughed. "I promise. Now, I better go change. I'm filling in for one of the hostesses at the restaurant this afternoon."

"Oh, I forgot. You work too much, you know."

Blair grinned. "Thank goodness I love my job. I'm blessed that way."

"Yes, we are at that."

When she was alone, Jillian studied the large room. What she'd proposed for Darlene was already over the top. Golden tablecloths, cream candles and cream roses, and crystals draped from the ceilings. And more…it was going to be spectacular. Jillian opened her wedding book and gazed over at the wedding board that she'd prepared months ago when they'd come in and booked the wedding. All of this had been preplanned and was ready to implement. The sudden turn of events was unexpected. She wondered whether Darlene was simply having cold feet. If so, they were the coldest feet Jillian had ever seen.

Needing a little fresh air herself, Jillian left the building and walked out along the swan lagoon and paused to watch them glide past.

"Watch out!" someone shouted. She turned around on the narrow walkway just in time to see a huge mass of fur and flapping lips crashing down the path. It barked loudly and then barreled into her. Jillian lost her balance, staggered backward with the weight of the dog and then fell backward into the small, shallow canal.

Sputtering and drenched, she sat up as the huge dog splashed in the water beside her. She looked up to see, of all people, Ryan jog into the water.

"Are you okay?" he asked.

She pushed her mass of hair out of her face, still not sure how she'd ended up in the water. "I think so. Where did this dog come from?"

Ryan offered her his hand. And she took it, instantly feeling the tug of attraction despite being dripping wet. He smiled as he pulled her up. "We received a call that there was a huge dog running loose on the beach. That animal has been causing havoc out there. You should see all the overturned picnic baskets and umbrellas lying broken behind him. And he made it to you and look at him. He's calm as a lamb now."

She was still breathing hard from falling as she looked down to find the huge, hairy white dog sitting on its haunches in the three feet of water. He grinned up at them; his tongue hung lazily to one side as his long tail zigged back and forth across the water.

She laughed. "You have no shame." She slapped her thighs to encourage the dog to come out of the water. "Come on, come out of the water." And he did; he lumbered out, dripping, and placed his wet head on Jillian's knee. She petted him and looked up at Ryan. "Any idea who he belongs too?"

"Let's see." He reached down and turned the tag on the dog's collar over. "His name is Roscoe and he belongs to…" Ryan chuckled. "Well, I'll be." He looked up. "He belongs to Kevin Donald Price."

"I know that name—oh! It's the little boy with the apple bobbing."

"Yes, it is. There's a phone number and an address. I think I'll run him over there instead of calling."

They were standing close and she realized for a few minutes they were back to not being uncomfortable with each other. The grocery store had been so bad. She'd wanted so badly to reach out to him but held back.

"Do you want to come with me? I can run you by your house so you can change. Unless you're going to finish your day wearing that look."

He'd taken hold of Roscoe's collar and held the monster pooch in place.

She started to decline but she did need to change. "Sure. That would be nice. And it will be fun seeing Kevin reunited with his dog."

Roscoe chose that moment to shake the water from his coat and sprayed them both.

"Oh, man," Ryan said. "That was half the bay coming off him."

"Tell me about it. I'm soaked again."

Minutes later, they climbed into his Windswept Bay SUV. He put the dog into the back while Jillian used towels she'd grabbed from the pool's towel cabana.

"I can't wait to take a shower. Do you have time for me to do that?"

"I have all the time you need. I'll make calls while you're showering."

She didn't live far from the resort and within moments, they pulled into her driveway. She had to give him directions but he had no trouble getting there.

"Here you go." He parked and they got out. Roscoe stuck his big head out of the window and barked. Ryan rubbed his head. "Stay put, buddy. This isn't your stop."

Ryan hadn't rolled it all the way down, not taking any chances in the dog getting loose again.

"I won't be long. You're welcome to come inside."

"I'll call Levi and let him know what's going on. I have to tell you, the last time I chased someone through the bushes, it was a drug dealer. It felt kind of weird chasing a dog."

She smiled tentatively. "Are you adjusting to the job?" She hadn't talked to Levi much over the last couple of weeks but she'd heard that Ryan was working.

"It's different. It's good."

She nodded and headed inside. There was no denying that she was glad to see Ryan. He looked so good, though he could have looked terrible and she would have thought the same thing. She had to be careful.

She had to be very careful.

Ryan had to be careful. *Very careful.*

He had chased Roscoe around the resort and never dreamed the chase would end the way it ended. He'd called Levi on the radio and then he'd phoned Kevin's mother. She was so relieved and assured him that from here on out he would be Kevin's hero.

When he was done, he was tempted to go into Jillian's home just so he could see it. He'd wanted to see her, to hear her voice but other than the night they'd run into each other at the grocery store, he'd avoided her.

He'd needed to give her space and if he was around her, that would have been impossible. Roscoe had changed that.

Ryan leaned up against the SUV and looked at Roscoe. "Yep, this is your fault. I have to play my cards right. Or she might keep running."

Roscoe cocked his head and his black eyes looked sympathetically at Ryan.

"I tell you, though," he said to the dog. Yes, Ryan acknowledged that he might have a problem, having a conversation with the dog. "She looked amazing…even dripping wet and with her mascara smudged, it took all my willpower to act like everything was cool. I have to be cool."

The door opened and Jillian walked outside. Ryan groaned. And so did Roscoe, as if understanding what Ryan was going through. Her hair was still damp from the shower and a slight curl softened it around her face. She wore simple white jeans and a soft blue blouse but she could have been wearing a little black dress and heels and she couldn't have been more beautiful to him.

"Sorry it took so long. I didn't take time to dry my hair."

"It's okay. Me and Roscoe here have been

bonding."

She chuckled, a soft tinkling glass sound that caused his insides to melt and his heart to hammer. "I hope you're going to be okay giving him back to Kevin," she teased as he opened her door for her.

"I'll manage. And may I say, you do clean up well."

Their eyes met. "Thank you," she said softly.

"Just stating the facts, ma'am."

He closed the door and berated himself all the way around the vehicle. *That was not cool. She'd run if he pushed.*

Her heart was clutched so tight that she had almost told him she would stay home. But she hadn't been able to do that. So here she was, riding beside him across town to a neighborhood that was just a few blocks from the beach.

They didn't need an address to know when they were at Kevin's house. The little boy stood in the yard and Roscoe barked and howled as he saw him.

"I think these two belong together," she said. "He must have just gotten lost and maybe was hunting for Kevin, because it's obvious they go together."

"I think you're right." He stopped the SUV and cut the engine. They got out as Kevin raced toward them.

His mother walked down from the porch. "Slow down, Kevin."

But the kid wasn't listening as Ryan opened the door. Roscoe dove from the car and met his human on two bounds.

Ryan stood beside her, their shoulders touching. She looked up at him. "So sweet," she said. "Feels good, doesn't it?"

"Yeah, it does."

"Thank you, Ryan," Kevin called as he looked up from hugging his huge dog. "I thought I'd lost him forever and forever." The little boy came and wrapped his arms around Ryan's knees. "You're the best." He looked up at Ryan. "I didn't know you were a policeman."

Ryan placed a hand on Kevin's head. "I am. And

I'm glad I could help you and Roscoe get back together."

Kevin sniffed. "Thank you. My daddy gave me Roscoe when he was a puppy. He means the world to me. And I was just praying and praying God would bring him back to me. And you did."

Ryan knelt. "Where's your daddy?"

Kevin looked down. "He's in heaven."

"Oh," Ryan said. "I'm real sorry."

"Thank you. Do you want to play with me and Roscoe? I have a fort in the backyard."

"Sure," Ryan said without hesitation and then looked at her. "I'll be back."

"Take your time," she assured him, reaching out and giving his arm an encouraging squeeze. He covered her hand with his and squeezed; then he followed the boy and the dog through a side gate and they disappeared around the house.

Kevin's mother watched too. Her arms were crossed and she was very still. "Thank you both for bringing him home. We went to the beach and left Roscoe at home but the gate must not have been latched good. He was gone when we came home. Kevin loves that dog so much." She had tears in her eyes. "It's the only thing he has left of his daddy…"

"He has you too." Jillian wrapped an arm around the woman, feeling as though she needed a hug. "I'm Jillian."

"I'm Jessica, and I really needed that hug."

"Me too. That was a tearjerker."

"Ryan is amazing. Kevin has talked about him ever since Thanksgiving. He has no idea how much he helped Kevin that day. Your resort too. We had to leave our friends and family and move here for my job recently and it's hard with the holidays. Coming out for the festival kept us busy."

"Oh, I am so glad we could help. And Ryan is just Ryan. I think that Kevin can have a buddy any time he needs one."

A few minutes later, Ryan walked back to them, with Kevin on his shoulders. Roscoe trailed them with his tail wagging.

"This is a great kid you've got here. I just started at the police department. Bring him by and we'll give him a tour. I also told him I'd give him a ride in the police car."

"Please, Mom."

"Yes. Thank you, I'll do it."

Minutes later, they drove away. She and Jessica had made plans to go to lunch.

When Ryan reached the stop sign, he didn't move. And then he turned left and headed toward the beach. He pulled to a halt in a parking space and then he reached across the car seat and took her hand. "Can we please talk?"

"I'd like that. I'd like that a lot."

Ryan led Jillian across the sand to the edge of the water. They didn't say anything as they walked but he felt a peace as he turned to her. "Jillian, I love you. I do. With all my heart. And I can understand if you've turned me down because you don't love me. But I can't take you turning me down because you think you could be depriving me of children."

"But I saw you with Kevin. You need children of

your own."

"I need *you*. I want *you*." He took her in his arms. "This is killing me. I'm not going anywhere. And one day we will have children. And we will love them, and cherish them no matter how we are blessed with them."

Jillian stared up at him, her expression softening. And tears glistened.

"I've done a lot of thinking in the last two weeks and I believe you are protecting me. You would sacrifice your happiness for mine if you thought that's what was in my best interest."

She stiffened as he leaned forward and gently kissed her right jaw. "You can't deny it, can you?" he murmured against her soft skin and then moved to kiss her left jaw. "Don't keep me on hold, Jillian. Don't keep our life together on hold."

"Ryan," she whispered. "I couldn't live with myself if you ever had any regrets."

His heart broke as he looked into her kind, sweet, loving eyes. "If you only knew how much I love you, you would know that the only regret I'll ever have is if

I have to live it without you as my wife."

"Oh, Ryan."

"Do you love me?"

"So much. I think I've always loved you."

"And that makes me the luckiest man alive."

Jillian's heart thundered at Ryan's words and as he lowered his lips to hers, she finally believed him…but she couldn't help herself from asking one more time, "You're sure?"

He laughed and swung her into his arms; she laughed. "Ryan."

"Jillian, stop overthinking this. You and me are where our home begins, with *our* love. Now please tell me you'll marry me. And marry me soon."

"Yes, I'll marry you." A joy filled her and she knew everything he'd said was right.

"Thank you," he yelled, looking heavenward, and then he kissed her like she'd never been kissed before…and she knew he was right. Their home and happiness began together.

Excerpt from

WITH THIS RING

Windswept Bay, Book Six

CHAPTER ONE

"Hurry, Momma. Drive faster."

Jessica Price shot a glance in the rearview at her six-year-old son. He was tiny for his age and looked so very small in the back seat. "I'm going the speed limit, young man. What's your hurry, anyway?" She knew what it was, but asked him anyway, glad to see his beaming smile again.

"It's show-and-tell and I have the best one of anybody," he exclaimed, bouncing in his seat belt.

Kevin had been excited ever since the day before when Deputy Ryan Locke, and his wife Jillian, had picked Kevin up and given him a ride in a Windswept Bay police SUV decked out with lights and siren. Kevin had been in heaven.

Ryan had promised him the ride before Christmas. But then Ryan and Jillian got married, and then Kevin had gotten ill. And then the holidays had taken precedence and there just hadn't been time for Ryan to fulfill his promise until yesterday. She'd been thrilled watching Kevin's joy as the man he'd connected with at Thanksgiving had strapped him into the backseat of his cop car and taken him for a ride. She didn't want Kevin to grow up and be thrilled to ride back there but for a little boy, it was one of the most exciting days of his life. It showed in his eyes as he'd looked at Ryan. It had been one more reminder to her that her son had no man, alive, to call Daddy and he so desperately wanted one.

He'd made that clear at Christmas.

But that was a hard thing, because she wasn't ready to think about marrying again. So for Ryan to come through on his promise after the Christmas they'd just had was a huge thing for her as well as for Kevin.

Ryan and Jillian had given Kevin a ride to the police station for a tour. And it had been there that he'd met Jillian's brother, Chief of Police Levi Sinclair. Kevin had talked nonstop about him.

It was obvious that he, too, had been kind to Kevin because, to her son's delight, the chief of police had agreed to come to the school today to be Kevin's show-and-tell in class.

It was the perfect distraction for him from what had happened over the holidays and seeing Kevin his happy self again made her happy. She would have to thank the chief because it was a welcomed difference from the quieter child Kevin had been since being so disappointed about not getting his Christmas wish. Her poor son.

They'd driven from Windswept Bay back home during the two-week holiday to spend Christmas with their family. With a six-year-old and Roscoe, their huge dog, it had been a long drive from Florida to

Kansas. The drive must have given Kevin time to come up with his heart-wrenching plan of asking Santa and God for a new daddy for Christmas!

He'd been one highly disappointed child when a new daddy had not been waiting for him underneath the Christmas tree on Christmas morning.

She sighed even now, thinking about it. She hadn't known how to help him. She wasn't ready to find a husband. Adam had only been dead two years. She needed time…though she certainly didn't want her little boy growing up without a daddy and nor would Adam want that. Her sweet husband had grown up without a dad and knew what it felt like. He would want her to remarry, for both Kevin and herself. But her heart…her heart was not ready.

And so this morning, as she drove to school with Kevin bouncing with excitement, she was happy. Maybe this was the start of a good new year after all.

They'd made it through one more Christmas without Adam, and as hard as it was, she knew they would make it…he would want it that way and he would want her to be strong. And she had been. Taking this job in Florida, so far away from her family, had been part of her determination to move forward. To stand on her own two feet.

She pulled into the parking lot of the school and smiled over the seat at Kevin. "We're here. Are you happy now?"

He grinned as he unbuckled his seat belt. "Oh yeah, this is going to be the greatest day of my life! All my friends are going to be so jealous." He grabbed the door handle.

"Hey, hold on there. You know not to open that door before I get out of the car." Her warning had him stopping before he jumped out of the backseat.

"Yes, ma'am. But could you please hurry?"

She laughed, grabbed her purse and got out of the car. The kid was going to run her ragged before her time.

Levi Sinclair stood outside the elementary school building. His phone rang and he pulled it from its clip on his belt. The ID showed that it was Jillian. He was in this fix because of her. She and Ryan had brought Kevin to tour the office and the cute little guy had been curious and excited and had asked Levi all kinds of questions. Levi had answered every one of them as Jillian and Ryan had stood in the doorway of his office and grinned while they watched. And then Kevin had asked him to come to his class today for show-and-tell. Levi hadn't been able to say no.

"Hey," he said, after accepting the call. His sister's soft chuckle greeted him.

"I called to remind you about Kevin's class this morning, but I can hear the angst in your voice so I'm assuming you're on your way."

He scowled. "I'm standing outside the school now. And stop laughing. You got me into this. You and my new deputy. I think you knew Kevin was going to ask me to do this. As a matter of fact, I bet you and your husband might have set me up."

Jillian chuckled again. "He did ask Ryan to do it when we were riding around in the SUV. But, Ryan just told him that the police chief would really be impressive to show off for his class. And he was right, this is a good thing."

"I'm glad you think so."

"Don't be nervous—you'll do fine."

"I'm not nervous," he denied, but in truth, he was a little. He'd never been comfortable when talking to kids and usually sent one of his deputies for things like this.

Levi liked kids; he just wasn't good with them. Which was why he'd been surprised when Kevin had taken his hand and had him come on the station tour with them. The freckled faced kid looked younger than a first grader and had chattered excitedly the whole time asking all kinds of questions. He had a great sense of humor and had Levi and Ryan laughing several times. There had been no way Levi could say no to helping him out.

"You were great with Kevin yesterday and he really enjoyed the time you spent with him. I just want to say good luck. Kevin needs this attention. And his mother, Jessica, is a sweetheart. You'll meet her. She's one of Kevin's teachers."

"Okay, well, I better get in there."

"Go and have a good time." She laughed and ended the call and he entered the school building.

Immediately Levi was transported back to his childhood, when he had been a student here at Windswept Bay Elementary. He'd been a rebel back then at the ripe old age of six. He and Ryan had, together, given the teachers the dickens. No one would have believed that he—or Ryan, for that matter—had grown up or would grow up to become police officers. Ryan's dad had been the police chief back then, and Mr. Locke and Levi's dad, Sam, had made many trips to the school's principal office to discuss their young reprobates.

Maybe that was the reason Levi had a little trouble coming back here for things like this. What if he saw a kid acting up? What was he supposed to say—watch out, if you keep acting like that you could grow up to become a police officer?

He laughed silently to himself as he reached room three. The door was open and he could see colorful tables with children looking toward the front of the room where a little girl was showing the class her turtle. A turtle might be far more interesting to a room of first graders than a police officer. Poor Kevin; this might be a no-win situation for the kid. And that suddenly bothered Levi.

Where was the teacher? Levi saw kids starting to notice him in the doorway and decided he needed to lean forward and look past the doorframe in order to see the rest of the room and find the teacher. Instead he waited until the little girl finished showing off her turtle—she reminded him of his sister Shar, who was a one-woman wonder when it came to rescuing endangered sea turtles. Heck, Shar would have been a huge hit for show-and-tell. Levi should have suggested her to Kevin instead of coming himself. The little girl set her turtle back in its box sitting at her feet. And then he started to lean forward, just as a pretty strawberry-blonde woman moved into view. Her blue eyes crinkled at the edges as she smiled at him.

"Hello, Chief Sinclair, it's so good of you to come. Just one moment please."

As she spoke, Levi wondered whether this was Kevin's mother. Jillian had said that she had been at the Thanksgiving Day Celebration that the Windswept Bay Resort his family owned put on each Thanksgiving. That was where Jillian and Ryan had first met Kevin and his mother. Then later they had rescued Roscoe, Kevin's dog, and returned it to the boy. That was when Ryan had promised to give Kevin a ride in the police vehicle, which had also turned into a tour of the station.

Studying the teacher, Levi realized he had seen her that day at the meal. She had been at the buffet line and he'd noticed then, like he was noticing now, that she had a soft beauty about her. He looked away, irritated with himself. He wasn't here to notice the teacher's beauty; he was here for Kevin. But when she glanced back to him briefly, her expression warm with welcome, he had a hard time focusing on anything but her.

"Class, we've been highly entertained by Clara and her turtle, Jeremiah. Thank you, Clara. You may sit down now."

Levi heard the smile in her voice and saw the twinkle in her eyes. An avalanche of attraction rumbled through him as she turned back to him and held out her hand.

"I am Jessica, Kevin's teacher and his very grateful mother." She leaned close so only he could hear her words. "Thank you so much for coming. It means the world to him. He's been so excited since yesterday when you agreed to show up."

He took her hand and yes, that attraction went up his arm like a forest fire eating up ground before he released her hand. "I'm glad to be here. Your son is quite a salesman."

"Yes, he is. Please, come in."

Levi stepped into the classroom and all the kids could see him now. He spotted Kevin at one of the tables with a look of complete exhilaration on his little face. The boy jumped to his feet and waved.

"Hi Levi-I mean Chief," he called.

Immediately Levi was glad he'd come. Ryan had told him that the boy had lost his father and Levi felt bad for him. "Hi Kevin."

Jessica chuckled. "Okay, Kevin, calm down. It's your turn for your show-and-tell time. I'll let you introduce your guest." And then smiling, she moved to the back of the room as Kevin raced full throttle to the front of the room and looked up at Levi with a gigantic grin from ear to ear.

"I knew you'd come," he gushed.

"Of course I came. You asked me, didn't you?"

Kevin nodded. "I did." He leaned forward and whispered, "I just had to see it to believe it." And then he stared at Levi for a long quiet moment.

"Kevin, introduce him," Jessica urged.

"Oh, yeah," he laughed and took Levi's hand and turned toward the class of about thirty-five.

Levi surveyed the room then. There was another woman at the back of the room who smiled as Jessica joined her. The kids were staring at him with varying degrees of interest and Levi suddenly felt very much like Jeramiah the turtle.

"Today, for my show-and-tell," Kevin said in a very serious tone, "I have brought Police Chief Sinclair. But I call him Levi, because he told me to the other day when he showed me the police station. It was really, really cool. But that's not why I brought him to be my show-and-tell." He grinned and looked up at Levi for a moment before dramatically looking back at the class. "I brought him to show you all that he is going to be my new daddy."

What? Levi nearly broke his neck as he looked from the class of suddenly alert, wide-eyed kids down to the boy grinning proudly at his classroom of peers; then the boy turned his face up and grinned at Levi with an expression of pure delight.

The boy had just told his classroom and his mother that Levi was going to be his new daddy…and he did not look like he was joking. Where had that come from?

Levi's gaze met Jessica's. Her mouth was open and she looked as if she'd just been hit with a bucket of ice water—then she turned red and hurried up the row of tables.

But Kevin was talking again, "When he's my daddy, we can all go to the station and he can take us on a tour then lock us all in jail cells and—"

Jessica interrupted him, "Kevin, um, that was interesting," she said in measured tones. "But you may sit down now."

"But, I'm not finished—" Kevin started.

Jessica held up a finger to stop him. "No sir," she said, firm but gentle. "You've had your time."

To his credit, the boy shot one last wistful look up at Levi and then headed back to his seat.

Levi, though stunned, noticed that the kid looked taller as he walked away.

Jessica turned toward him and a pale pink tint stained her cheeks. Her blue eyes seemed to ask for understanding. "I'm sorry," she said softly. "He's going through a tough time right now. I had no idea he planned to do that."

Levi had been trained for all types of trouble. Nothing had prepared him for this…it was awkward to say the least. And sadly a little heartbreaking. He felt for her and he felt for Kevin.

"It's okay," he assured her. "Since I'm here, can I say something to the kids?"

Relief flashed in her expression. "Yes, please, whatever you would like. The floor is yours. The children would be thrilled to hear something from you.

And maybe it would distract from what just happened," she said, continuing in the soft tones that they had been speaking in.

"That's exactly what I was thinking."

She turned back to the children who were now talking excitedly. "Calm down, everyone. Chief Sinclair wants to say a few words to all of you. Now please quiet down and give him the respect that he as our police chief and one of the men who protects us and our community deserves."

Levi watched her as she moved aside. She chose not to go to the back of the room this time but instead stood near the doorway.

"I think Kevin may have made a great suggestion for a field trip. I think I'll coordinate with Ms. Price for a tour of the police station for the classes and all of you kids can meet my deputies. That way when you see them on the streets, you will know them and know that they are your friends. And that if you ever need help, you can feel comfortable asking them." He was amazed at how the children stared at him with complete attention.

One of the boys in the front row raised his hand and Levi decided that questions from the kids might be a good option.

"You have a question?" He pointed at the kid; immediately, other hands went up around the room.

The little boy grinned. "When are you getting married?"

And then the questions started.

"When are you marrying Ms. Price?"

"My mom is not going to be happy," a little girl huffed. "She said she was going to marry you, Chief Sinclair. My mom said you were a hot hunk."

"My mama said she bet you kissed good," a little boy said and made a face. "That's gross."

"Class," Jessica gasped.

"Hold on, kids." Levi held up his hand, deciding maybe he should have left when he had the chance. How many of these kids' moms had talked about him? He glanced over at Jessica who looked as troubled as he felt.

"Class," she said, her voice tight. "Police Chief Sinclair and I are not getting married. And I would thank you for not spreading this around."

"But Kevin said so," someone declared.

"Yes, he did, but no. We are not getting married."

"I believe it's time for me to go." He told her.

The little girl whose mother had called him a hunk and wanted to kiss him jumped from her chair. "My mom is not going to be happy."

Levi did not even answer; he just got out of there as fast as his shoes would carry him. Show-and-tell had not been a good idea.

Not a good idea at all.

More Books by Debra Clopton

Windswept Bay Series

From This Moment On (Book 1)

Somewhere With You (Book 2)

With This Kiss (Book 3)

Forever and For Always (Book 4)

Holding Out For Love (Book 5)

With This Ring (Book 6)

With This Promise (Book 7)

With This Pledge (Book 8)

With This Wish (Book 9)

With This Forever (Book 10)

With This Vow (Book 11)

Check out Debra's Other Series

Cowboys of Dew Drop, Texas

Sunset Bay Romance

Texas Brides & Bachelors

New Horizon Ranch Series

Star Gazer Inn of Corpus Christi Bay

Cowboys of Ransom Creek

Texas Matchmaker Series

About the Author

Debra Clopton is a USA Today bestselling & International bestselling author who has sold over 3.5 million books. She has published over 81 books under her name and her pen name of Hope Moore.

Under both names she writes clean & wholesome and inspirational, small town romances, especially with cowboys but also loves to sweep readers away with romances set on beautiful beaches surrounded by topaz water and romantic sunsets.

Her books now sell worldwide and are regulars on the Bestseller list in the United States and around the world. Debra is a multiple award-winning author, but of all her awards, it is her reader's praise she values most. If she can make someone smile and forget their worries for a few hours (or days when binge reading one of her series) then she's done her job and her heart is happy. She really loves hearing she kept a reader from doing the dishes or sleeping!

A sixth-generation Texan, Debra lives on a ranch in Texas with her husband surrounded by cattle, deer, very busy squirrels and hole digging wild hogs. She enjoys traveling and spending time with her family.

Visit Debra's website and sign up for her newsletter for
updates at: www.debraclopton.com

Check out her Facebook at:
www.facebook.com/debra.clopton.5

Follow her on Instagram at: debraclopton_author

or contact her at debraclopton@ymail.com

9 781949 492347